A HARLOT'S TALE

A HARLOT'S TALE

Word of His Mouth Publishers
Mooresboro, NC

ISBN: 978-1-941039-06-9
Printed in the United States of America
©2019 Nishoni Harvey

Word of His Mouth Publishers
Mooresboro, NC 28114
www.wordofhismouth.com

Chapter 1

Mountain goats bounded through the field, their tan coats shimmering in the hot sun. Some of the males sported horns that were longer than they were tall. Their movements seemed majestic and peaceful. Their bleats fell softly on Rahab's ears. *Oh! To be a goat and be able to bound away from my troubles!*

The fields were full of wildflowers. A beautiful sea of purples, yellows, and blues. The gentle wind blew across them in waves, carrying with it their wondrous scent. It had a hypnotic effect on Rahab, reminding her of everything good, pure, and right.

She was drawn from her reverie by ear-piercing screams. A chill swept across her as she jerked her head toward the sound. Running as quickly as she could in the tall grass and flowers, she neared the old gnarled tree, tall from age and permanently bent and distorted from the winds and periodic lightning strikes, to where her frantic seven-year-old sister stood. *Maybe a snake?* As she rushed closer, she saw her baby brother, short for his age, lying on the hard ground holding his leg. *Why wasn't I paying more attention?*

"What happened, Emma?"

"Aliyan was climbing the tree and fell. I told him not to!" Her voice was quick and spastic.

Kneeling lightly beside Aliyan, Rahab looked over his little body. *Five years old is awfully young to break a leg, and it's all my fault!*

"Aliyan, can you move your leg?"

Big tears stained his flushed cheeks, causing a shimmer on his black skin. His breath came in short gasps as he slowly recovered from his crying. He nodded his head quietly. "Yes. Yes, I think so. It feels better now." He gingerly moved his leg back and forth, testing it.

"What happened, Aliyan?" Rahab was trying to sound firm but knew she was failing. She caressed his head, running her fingers through his hair in a comforting gesture.

He looked down, picking at the grass beside him.

"Aliyan?"

"I—I was climbing in the tree. I was climbing and fell." He continued to pick at the grass, refusing to look up.

"Aliyan! You know you're not allowed in the trees!" Searching his face, her demeanor softened. "I suppose I could let it go this time. Don't let it happen again."

"Thank you, Rahab!" He enthusiastically threw his slender arms around her neck and then tottered off to play.

Rahab walked slowly back to her work. She felt the warm sun upon her back as its rays gently caressed her sore muscles. She'd been harvesting flowers, many of their seeds edible, apples, olives and medicinal herbs, like Queen Ann's Lace, since late morning. Now her body was feeling it. Of course, having her eighteen-month-old sister strapped to her back didn't help either.

Rahab glanced at her three younger siblings again. *If only I had that much energy!* They were all eagerly gathering flowers "to make home pretty" and had been for as long as she'd been gathering food and herbs to add to their meager supply.

Jericho had two walls, a strong outer wall and a taller, much thicker inner wall. This offered Jericho two defenses against outside attacks. Rahab and the children usually stayed between the walls of Jericho, but Rahab had decided they'd travel outside the outer rim of the city today. She knew a change in scenery would be good for everyone.

She gazed compassionately at Hagdad, who looked almost like an exact duplicate of Rahab. She was flustered as she attempted to direct the children in an effort to keep them together. She had *just* turned thirteen years old, making her almost two years younger than Rahab. Her hair, dark as a moonless night, laid long down her back. It was the same color as her dark skin, which was a little darker than Rahab's. Her kinky locks were woven into many small braids, which was how most Jericho women and girls wore their hair. Her dark eyes and thick lashes made her eyes look too large for her face. She had long bony fingers and pointy elbows like Rahab did. She, like Rahab, looked too skinny with a waist that was too thin and a chest that was too large.

Rahab's mother loved to point out that the only difference between the two girls was in their facial features. Where Rahab had full, lush lips, perfect teeth, and rounded cheeks, Hagdad had pencil thin lips and a face that was marred with acne.

Their personalities were also completely opposite. Rahab was mature and responsible—the result of "playing Mama" for so many years. Hagdad, on the other hand, was whimsical and carefree.

3

The wonderful scent of wildflowers drew Rahab's attention back to her task. A fluffy white cloud, one of only a few in the bright blue sky, floated slowly across the sun, cooling Rahab a bit. She shivered, amazed at the quick change in temperature, but then it was that time of year—early summer. It had always amazed her how the temperature could change so drastically from moment to moment—boiling hot one second and so cool the next. She stood upright and looked around in appreciation for all Astarte had given them in creating such a beautiful world.

The song of six of her neighbors wafted toward her as they worked hard harvesting flax in the next field. Although she was thankful for the many healing capabilities it had, the food it provided, and for the fibers that were extracted to make the cloth for clothes, she still hated to see the beautiful blue flowers on the flax disappear as it was cut down for harvesting.

She gazed at the many palm trees, which cast so much cooling shade in the middle of the hot summer.

A bird flew overhead. She heard another, sitting in a nearby tree and singing its pretty song.

In the distance, men drew water from a spring for their cattle grazing nearby. There were many springs spread around the city, inside and outside the walls. They provided a certain beauty and supplied cool, clear water. The springs attracted many people of many different origins and colors to the city as they traveled through the land.

She didn't care for the strangers who came through Jericho. Strangers made her nervous. Most of them were good people, and she was told the money they spent was the majority of the income for many of the small businesses. Even her father's small fish shop profited well from the many strangers in the land. But some travelers were evil men who would kill, rape, or plunder at any opportunity.

Rahab hated going through the alleys or around corners that hid her from the view of the crowds and tried to avoid being alone at any cost. She often took longer routes and harder roads to avoid making herself vulnerable. She didn't mind the marketplace since there were lots of people there—not necessarily people to protect her, but people who would witness against anyone who committed a crime. Most people, even the worst people, wouldn't try to hurt someone in a crowd.

She had heard of a young woman that had taken a short cut through a dark alley in an attempt to make an appointment on time. She had been attacked by a group of drunken men. They had beaten her badly in just a few minutes. She was able to break free and rush toward the crowded streets. The group of men stayed hidden in the dark alley, away from the streets, and she had been spared by her wise move.

Other than the danger some of the strangers posed, Rahab loved Jericho—her Jericho. The small city was so engrossed in and encompassed by the worship of Astarte, the moon goddess, that the city, whose name meant, "Moon," was named in honor of the goddess. Jericho was the center of the worship of Astarte, and everything Astarte commanded was practiced in the city. The people of Jericho gave themselves wholly to Astarte, unlike other lands around them. Yes, she loved her Jericho. She loved her god.

She smelled fires being started to prepare the evening meal. *Fires! Supper! Late again!* Time had always been her archenemy. Whether she was washing her long and kinky jet-black hair, oiling her body until her dark-colored skin shone brightly, doing one of her many chores, or just loafing around doing nothing, time always eluded her. Today was no different.

"Aliyan! Emma! Hagdad! Bilba!" *Dummy. Bilba's on my back.* "Let's go!"

The setting sun was beginning to redden the sky. *Oh! I'm in so much trouble!* She knew that when she returned home, she'd receive the wrath of her domineering father. Again.

Jericho always seemed to loom over her whenever she entered the city. It always made her feel so small. At the same time, the immensity of the tall, thick walls awed her and made her feel safe and secure. Nothing could ever get through those walls—ever.

Walking through the tall wooden gates, which would be closing as soon as darkness fell completely, she looked at the majestically clad guards. She always appreciated the fact that they were there to keep her and her family safe. She loved their flashy attire and the rigidity of their stance. The only thing she disliked was the fact that they smelled horrible, like a mixture of dust, sweat, and horse.

Inside the walls, the city bustled with activity. People rushed to and fro, some searching for last-minute buys, some looking for yet another night of pleasure, and some rushing to get home before darkness fell. The heavy dust flooding the air filled her nose, almost choking her, as people pushed their way through the crowded streets and past her little group. *Why did they have to put the marketplace so close to the city gates?* The smell of food cooking inside the many homes made her stomach rumble. She heard pounding hooves, people shouting, and the rumble of chariot wheels, the sounds of yet another race being run on the top of the city walls.

On the side of the street sat the old lady who was always there—day in and day out—selling apples. Rahab didn't know her name but called her, as everyone else did, "the apple lady." She was kind to the apple lady, and, in return, the apple lady had always been kind to her. She would always remember something the apple lady had once said to her: "Take life by the horns, girl! You can have anything you want. You just have to work for it. Decide what you want, set a plan in motion, and don't quit until you get it!"

There was only one thing Rahab wanted. She wanted to live like the apple lady. Not selling apples in the marketplace, but she wanted to live free. Free of men and their tyranny. The apple lady stood up for herself. She was her own boss and took orders from no one. She took care of herself without the help of any man. If all men were like her father, and she believed they were, Rahab didn't want anything to do with any man. That especially included marriage, but she knew it would happen—eventually. Every woman in Jericho was condemned to marriage by the age of sixteen. *Stupid traditions.*

Rahab heard cows mooing, goats and sheep bleating, and pigs grunting. She couldn't see them, but she could hear and smell them. She wondered who would buy such disgusting creatures unless it was to butcher them immediately to provide meat for their family. The animals in the marketplace were covered in all kinds of nasty filth.

The light of the rising moon drew her attention. Astarte was happy tonight. She showed it by giving the blessing of a full and bright moon. Centered in front of the moon, outlined in its soft, white light, was a large, beautiful house. The house Rahab dreamed of owning one day. The most beautiful house on the top of the city walls. The dream that would never come true.

Remembering the apple lady's words, "You can have anything you want. You just have to work for it. Decide what you want, set a plan in motion, and don't quit until you get it," she rethought her "never" statement. Why shouldn't she be able to own that house?

She could work as hard to achieve her dreams as anyone else!

The house was made of mud bricks, just like every other house in the city, but it was different. The house was so old that the merciless sun had slowly faded the color of the bricks, making it very unique. The house was bigger and the walls taller than any other house in the city, at least in the parts of the city that Rahab knew. The windows were round instead of the normal square windows of the city. The roof had different levels making it look like many smaller houses had been built to touch one another and were joined to make one house. She loved the old house. She'd heard many people admire it. *I'm going to own that house. One day, that house will be mine.*

Rounding a corner, she and her siblings came upon a man and woman shamelessly sporting in the street. He had his hands all over her as they kissed passionately. Surely they realized she and the children were there, but they continued on anyway. *Stupid men. Always taking advantage of women. Taking advantage of every opportunity. Stupid harlots. They're just as bad. What brings a woman to such a low place where she so freely and unashamedly offers herself to men? Men. Pigs.*

Most harlots chose the dark alleys or inns to conduct their business in, another reason she avoided alleys, but this one unashamedly did it right out in the open. In front of everyone.

Corralling her siblings, she rushed them past the scene as quickly as she could but not quickly enough. The damage had already been done. They had seen the disgusting display and had many questions, questions they asked in innocence.

Aliyan, who was clinging tightly to her hand, looked up at her, a complex look on his face. "Rahab, what were they doing?"

"They were being bad."

"But, why, Rahab?"

"Because some people like to be bad."

Emma, who had been sheltered from the degradation for seven years, took a deep breath. "Why were they touching each other so?"

"Because that's what some bad people do."

"Rahab," Emma said to her, brow wrinkled. "I don't understand."

Rahab was getting more and more disgusted with what her siblings, her babies, had seen. Having raised the last three from birth, she'd kept them from seeing such filth. Until tonight.

"Enough questions," she said firmly. "Let's not talk about bad people and bad things anymore. Let's think about good things, like the beautiful moon Astarte has blessed us with tonight."

She saw her home in the distance. She couldn't see the mud bricks very well due to the darkness that had enveloped her and the children, but she knew what her home looked like by memory. The people who had built the house had done a rushed and poor job, so there were many chips in the bricks and places where whole chunks had fallen off. The house was still sturdy and strong, though unsightly.

Through the open windows, she could already hear her father yelling. She grimaced at what was to come. *This isn't going to be pretty.* The moon had crept higher into the sky, long past time for her to be home. The yelling quieted inside. *Great! He's seen me coming and is already planning what hateful words to use first.*

Leaning against the wall of the mud brick house, Rahab took a deep breath and tried to calm her nerves.

She didn't understand her reaction since she was usually so callous and unshakable when it came to her father's verbal abuse. She was usually so strong. She had to be for the children. If she didn't, who would be? No one. Not her mother. Not anyone else. No one. She had to be strong.

He used to be a wonderful father when she was a small child, but over the years, he had become more hostile and controlling due to one close call with the business. He'd come close to losing it several years ago. Very close to losing everything he had. His heart. His pride. His life. He came so close to the worst loss he could imagine, and it changed him. It made him the way he was now. As he grew more tyrannical, she grew more stubborn and rebellious toward him.

"Children, stay out here until I tell you to come in." Rahab desperately hoped they would listen. They usually did. She took a sleeping Bilba off her back and handed her to Hagdad. "Careful with her. Try not to wake her."

As soon as she came through the door, Rahab knew something was amiss. She couldn't place her finger on it, but something wasn't right. Her mother was slumped in a light-colored wooden chair at the large table, her face buried in her work-worn hands. Normally, her father's tirades pushed her mother into uncontrollable crying. Then she would retreat to the corner by the window—her corner, which she sat in often, blocking out pain, the world, and consequently, her children.

Her father was pacing, his hands clutched behind his back, and his head bent forward like he was searching the floor. His normal behavior after a tirade was to storm out of the house in a fit of rage, screaming obscenities as he went. No, something was wrong—very wrong.

"Mother? Father?" Rahab took a shaky, deep breath to steady her nerves. *Has someone died? No, that doesn't explain the fit of fury.* The fire in the hearth had been allowed to burn down to grey coals, and dinner wasn't even started. *Odd. Mother never lets the fire go out… even on the hottest of days, and dinner is always on time.* She took another deep breath as her eyes darted back and forth between her parents, who now stared at her. Sorrow—or regret—was etched upon their faces, neither daring to look her in the eye. This wasn't about her being so late. This was about something else. What had she done?

Rahab winced at the deep bruises on her mother's face. *The latest abuse, no doubt.* "What's wrong?" She feared the worst. As she stumbled over the simple phrase, her words caught in her throat, her voice sounding high-pitched and quivering to her ears.

Her mother slowly rose from her seat and dragged herself off to her corner, her retreat in every emotional crisis. She turned her face from Rahab and stared through the open window at the silhouettes of other people's homes—happy homes.

Rahab slowly shifted her gaze to her father, hoping that he'd be more help. "Father?" her voice cracked.

"Well…" He paused to clear his throat. She'd never seen him act this way before. He was always so in control. Today, he seemed almost nervous. This worried Rahab even more. Was it truly nervousness she saw or was he trying too hard to act and cover something up? Something. But what? He shifted his gaze around, looking everywhere but at her.

"You're getting married next Saturday," her father said; as he said it, his eyes traveled to her face, gauging her reaction.

She felt the floor shift beneath her as her world came to a sudden stop. *Married? What?* She'd thought she had at least thirteen more months before marriage would be forced upon her. Women weren't required to marry until sixteen.

Rahab took a step forward so she could grasp the back of the closest chair for stability. She looked back up at her father. His façade was starting to fall apart. He was smiling, only a hint of a smile, small, yet noticeable. It had all been a ploy! The nervous pacing, the look of concern and worry, all of it! She'd thought, for just a moment, that he was truly sorry, that he really felt for her, just this once. She was wrong. It was just a game to him—another of his twisted, demented games. *Of course. Controlling monster.*

An evil smile spread across his face. He crossed his arms in front of him and puffed out his chest. He took a big step toward her as his eyes narrowed and his smile deepened. "You're marrying *Yassib*."

The name hit her like a ton of bricks. Her world began to spin. *No.* She wouldn't let him win. She'd stay on her feet and even appear collected.

She knew well why he'd placed emphasis upon the name. Yassib was a self-serving pig, and everyone knew it. He'd had it in for Rahab since they'd first met in the marketplace three years ago. That was the day she'd smashed an over-ripe mango in his face for calling her a scrawny no-good. Only Astarte knew what he'd do to her once he had her legally under his control, when he had her in a place where he could do *anything* he wanted.

"No!" She spat vehemently, regaining her composure. "No, I won't do it!"

She looked defiantly at her father, her dark eyes narrowed, and her head held high. She removed her hands from the back of the chair, stood to her full height of five feet six inches, and pursed her lips together, daring him to make her. She knew he would expect rebellion from her. She'd always stood up to him. She was the only one who dared try. Maybe this was how he planned to finally put her in her place and show her who was boss.

A full smile spread across his lips, a smile that didn't reach his eyes. It was the smile he used when he knew he had you exactly where he wanted you—under his control. *Monster.*

"Well now," he said, his voice was sickeningly sweet. "I don't see as *you* have any choice."

He was right. She didn't have a choice. Not yet. Surely there was a way out. She just had to find it. She *had* to. She'd find a way out if it killed her.

"You'd better get your little self up to the temple," her father said, "and await your turn to serve Astarte." Every woman was required to freely offer her body to be used once for one man's pleasure before she was allowed to marry.

The temple! Yes! That might be it! Someone would have to choose her over the hundreds of other women sitting in the courtyard before she'd be eligible to marry Yassib. Some women sat in the courtyard every day for years before they were chosen. Maybe she would get lucky. She wasn't the most beautiful girl in Jericho. She was too skinny.

Chapter 2

Rahab watched as the morning sun rose in all its splendor. The colors dazzled the world as they danced across the sky in a great symphony. *How can the day start so perfectly with a sunrise like that on a day like today—the day that I'm being forced to give of myself so freely? The day I make my trek to the temple?*

"Good morning." Her mother's voice was sad and monotone. Rahab secretly wished the depression oozing from her was because she felt sad for Rahab, but that wasn't the truth. It would never be the truth. Her mother was too busy feeling sorry for herself. "What has you up so early?"

"I never slept."

"Excited about your temple journey today?" Her mother's melancholy voice grew grimmer. Perhaps she *did* feel sorry for her! But, then again, how could she ask such a question?

Rahab sighed and slowly turned back toward the blossoming sky, shoulders slumping and back bowed, pretending to be taking joy in it. Was *this* how her mother felt all the time? Did she, too, feel like the world was colored in drab grays and like it held nothing for her? No wonder she sat around staring into space for so much of the day.

She turned back to her mother to answer her question, to pour out her heart to her, to tell her how she really felt, how she was truly devastated and broken inside. She turned to tell her, but she was gone. *Sounds right.* Taking a deep breath, she reached for the sky, trying to stretch out her weary muscles. *Why me?* Hanging her head, tears tried to flow again.

Rahab could hear some of her father's favorite words reverberating in her mind. "Useless. Tears do you absolutely no good. They make you look weak. Keep your tears to yourself."

Might as well get on with it.

She looked at her home as though she would never see it again. The hopelessness that engulfed her suggested that she truly might not. *Maybe I could just run away and hide!* But she knew it was useless to even ponder that.

Slowly passing the old sycamore trees at the end of her yard, she felt like she was passing the point of no return. The trees meant no turning back, not that she could if she wanted to. Slowly, she inched her way past the sycamores, panting in anxiety, trying not to hyperventilate. Once past them, she took a breath, held her head high, and trudged on toward the temple. She would not allow her father, who was undoubtedly watching from a window, to think he'd won. She wouldn't give him the satisfaction of seeing her distress.

The relentless sun seared through her clothes as she walked, making her dark skin feel hot as a burning iron. The heat was stifling, almost choking her. She was thankful for the many shade-bearing palm trees she passed beneath. Jericho, the city of palms. The bustling around the city, many of the people on their way to or from one of the many springs, helped to keep her mind distracted. Weaving in and out through the throng slowed her. People pushed past. The lowing of oxen and the jarring of carts filled her ears. She kept plugging on, her tired feet seeming to know where to go and carrying her onward of their own volition.

Rahab paused. Her eyes grew wide. Her jaw dropped open. Her breath caught in her throat. The temple of Astarte stretched before her. She was, as always, awed by its splendor. The magnificence of its size astounded her. It rose high above her and stretched before her almost as far as she could see. The large rocks that made up its walls were fitted together in a perfect puzzle. Several of the large rocks were engraved with holy animals and plants that represented Astarte, and many were engraved with golden words that conveyed her many attributes. The masses of people aside, the temple truly was beautiful, just like the goddess it was built for.

Astarte was so interesting. She had so many opposites: goddess of war and sensual love, death and life, joy and tears, fire and water, positive and negative, fair dealing and enmity, and the extinguishing and lighting of fires. Astarte was the destroyer of and giver of life, and she fought fiercely to protect her people, even from other gods. She was truly worthy of worship.

Rahab slowly stole through the welcoming pillars, each one a large, white lion, into the temple courtyard. A nude statue of Astarte graced the middle of the courtyard. She stood on the backs of two life-size lions. She wore fine earrings and a beautiful necklace. She stood tall, a crescent moon above her and a hook-shaped twisted knot of reeds in her hands.

Making her way to the sacred plot of Astarte, Rahab saw many women already seated, waiting for a stranger to come by and choose her for his partner. *Maybe I* will *be lucky. With this many women waiting to be chosen, I'm sure to be here quite a while.*

She spied a basket of short, brown cords, woven from the dried stalks of the many wildflowers found around Jericho. She'd almost forgotten she needed one. It was a necessary part of the uniform of a woman in her position. *I wonder where this silly tradition came from. The silliest traditions tend to last the longest.* Tying her crown of cord upon her head, she sat down as far away from the others as she could. Perhaps if she were far off, men would miss her altogether. A prayer couldn't hurt. She muttered a familiar prayer; *"To the Lady of Heaven and Earth, who receives prayers, who harkens to the petitions, who accepts beseechings; to the merciful goddess who loves righteousness; Look upon me, O Lady, so that through thy turning toward me the heart of thy servant may become strong."*

She settled in for a long wait, but before she could even get comfortable, money was tossed into her lap, showing she had been chosen.

"I invite you in the name of Mylitta." Rahab recognized the all too familiar voice.

Please, Astarte. No! It was Yassib. His sandals were dirty and worn. Just like his wretched soul. His blue robe fell just above his sandals. He had a white sash tied around his loins. The top of his robe fell open, showing his collarbone and the very top of his bared chest. His neck was long and thick, well-defined muscles gently rounded at the sides. Her gaze swept up to his face. It truly was beautiful, drawing the attention of every girl he passed, but the sneer on his face at that moment distorted it into a hateful mask. His shorn hair, dark as it was, looked almost blue in the sunlight. His tall stature, a full head and shoulders above everyone else, towered above her. Menacing.

Rising from her seat, Rahab followed him to the bench, as she was forced to do by the law of Astarte. *So humbling, already, but right here in front of everyone and with* him*? Why me?* If she had to be chosen, why not by someone else? Anyone else?

"Lay down and lift your skirts," he commanded harshly, but Rahab didn't move. "Didn't you hear me?" he demanded. He lifted his hand to strike her, the back of his hand, attached to a muscular arm.

She moved quickly into position, and he climbed on top of her.

It was done and over within seconds, but to Rahab, it seemed like it took forever. The pain was intense. He seemed to know that, and that seemed to bring him pleasure.

"Now go home, woman. We marry one week from today."

She sank even lower in her depression. Her plan hadn't worked. The wedding wouldn't be delayed. She would have to marry the abusive Yassib. Dark despair engulfed her.

The chime of tinkling bells sounded behind her, mixed with the sweet sound of giggling. She looked up just in time to see a young man leading a completely nude young woman into a chamber. *Temple prostitute. How do they get over their humiliation? Maybe Astarte gives them a divine gift since they give themselves in that way to serve her.* The young woman gave her an idea. Many girls willingly became temple prostitutes to serve Astarte in the highest form possible and to bring honor, health, happiness, and prosperity to their family, which was what Astarte promised. If Rahab became a temple prostitute, it would be her way out of marrying Yassib. It would also be a good mark on her family.

Rahab turned and walked into the temple.

Stepping over the threshold, she was overwhelmed. The outside beauty of the temple failed in comparison of that on the inside. The ceilings were high and vaulted; there were broad pillars throughout the temple holding it up. She noticed that each pillar was different, each depicting a different animal: snakes, serpents, dragons, cows, scorpions, and more, all animals that depicted Astarte.

She stooped down to look at a picture etched in brass that was repeated along the bottoms of the smooth walls all the way around the inside of the temple. It was a nude female with long wings, sharp talons, and a beautiful headdress and horns. There were two owls standing beside her, and she seemed to be balancing the top of a scale. Such a beautiful depiction. She gingerly reached out to touch it.

Someone cleared their throat behind her. "May I help you?"

Rahab jumped. Turning around, she saw an older woman clothed in a long, flowing, see-through gown. *What's the use of that?*

"Can I help you with something, young lady?" She was starting to get impatient. Rahab could hear it in her voice.

Rahab smelled a strong, sweet scent—a very pretty scent—coming from the woman. Or was it? She couldn't remember if she'd smelled it before the woman's sudden appearance.

"I—I come to present myself to be a temple prostitute for the glory of Astarte," she managed to stutter out.

The woman slowly looked Rahab over from head to toe and then back up again, assessing her through her scrutiny. Her face remained the same—all business. "Come with me."

Rahab followed, almost gawking at the beauty all around her. A beautiful, golden seven-pointed rosette, one of the many flowers that represent the goddess, graced each door. She wondered if the rosettes were putting off the scent. She knew it was impossible, but she didn't know where else the beautiful smell that filled the air could be coming from.

Ahead, she saw a wide doorway with a carved mantle. In the very center of the doorway hung a golden sun. On either side stood two very different statues of Astarte. On the left, she was clad in armor, riding a lion-drawn chariot as she hunted both animals and humans. On the right, she was a temple prostitute with glad eyes, the goddess of desire whose beloved song was known to be sweeter far than honey, sweet cream, or wine. Astarte, Morning and Evening star, the goddess of war and of sex, the great goddess Astarte.

Rahab felt the breeze upon her flushed skin. She glanced toward the open window through which the cool breeze had come. Eight-pointed stars, golden with many red rubies set along their borders, were placed on either side of the window. Rahab looked and saw that every window was the same.

Two date palms, representing the living tree—the tree of life and creation, were set in the corners of the chamber they had entered. They were planted in golden pots decorated with many precious gems. The sunlight reflected off the gems, momentarily blinding Rahab. She wanted to touch the artistic impression of the animals that graced the walls behind them. The animals, which resided in the tree of life in the spiritual realm, were hemmed in by larger pictures of the birds of the Upper World and the snake of the mysterious Underworld.

The copper stars, embedded with quartz crystals and hanging around the tops of the tall walls, made Rahab think of the night sky and the many stars that seemed to play music to her on the clear nights that she could sneak out without her father noticing.

Her father. He'd kill her if he knew what she was about to do. She'd heard him swear many times that he'd never have a harlot for a daughter. Wasn't a temple prostitute simply a glorified harlot? It didn't matter. She *had* to do it. She couldn't marry Yassib. She just couldn't.

"Wait here." The woman she'd been following entered a door to the right.

Rahab took in the beauty of a large basin set before her. It was made of pure silver; covered in gold stars and copper moons, and rimmed with rubies, sapphire, diamonds, and other precious stones she didn't know the names of. She let her hand brush the cool water, barely disturbing the surface. She peered in to see her reflection and startled as she noticed a young woman standing behind her.

The woman was dressed exactly like Rahab's guide had been. "Come with me, and I'll take you to the chamber where you'll sign the pact to become a holy temple prostitute."

As she followed behind her, Rahab began to second guess herself. Could she really go through with this? Did she really *want* too? No, she didn't want to, but she had no other choice! She had to or likely die at the hands of Yassib.

The sight of the men sporting with the temple prostitutes in the courtyard had sickened her. She remembered seeing the whore on her way home with the children only the night before. She had wondered what had brought the whore so low. Well, this was her lowest point. Yassib—no, her life—was her reason for entering into this pact. She had to do it. Even now, Yassib was controlling her, but at least it was in a way of her choosing.

Rahab bumped into her guide. *Oops! Stupid, she stopped walking!* She looked at Rahab with that same all-business look that the other woman had given her. Rahab shivered as a chill ran through her. Is this what she'd be like seven years from now?

"This way." Her guide motioned with her hand, and Rahab stepped through the open door. Inside, it was dark, lit only by two candles. There were no windows, no breeze. The air was stale. Between the two candles sat a wrinkled old woman behind a table. Her shoulders were slumped with age. Her eyes were deep-set and dark. Her hands were shaking. Her fingers were deformed. Her hair was silver and braided close to her head.

"State your purpose." The woman looked at Rahab, appearing to look through her.

"I, um," Rahab stumbled over her words. *Get it together!* "I wish to become a temple prostitute to the glory of Astarte." *Why do they make themselves so intimidating?*

"Very well. Come." *Great. Another walk to nowhere.* But the woman didn't leave the room. She simply took faltering steps to the other side of the room, taking one of the burning candles with her. Its flame jumped and weaved with the shaking of her hand. The light cast eerie shadows on the wall.

Why didn't they put windows in this room?

"Are you sure this is what you want to do? You realize this is a seven-year commitment and that there is no getting out early?" Her voice sounded monotone like she had repeated those words a hundred times and said them now in her sleep. "You realize that once you make your choice, it's done?"

"Yes." *I don't want to do this!* "I understand."

"Very well. By taking this oath of service, you promise to uphold the laws of Astarte. You promise to serve her in any way she sees fit. You will help men who come to worship Astarte in their worship. As the goddess of sex and love, you will perform the duties of a temple prostitute to create a way, a channel of worship for these men. Your drive, your purpose, will be one thing and one thing only: to the glory of Astarte."

The woman looked at Rahab expectantly. *What does she want me to do?*

"I understand."

"Do you promise to uphold these statutes?" She sounded a little irritated.

"Oh! Yes, I promise."

"Very well." Why does she keep saying that?

The woman moved to the corner of the room where a small wooden table sat. There were intricate pictures of Astarte carved on the lip round about. In the center of the table stood a large pitcher, painted white with red roses and a small, earthen bowl painted green and white with figures of a naked Astarte pictured on it. In the bowl rested a budded red rose with a long, thornless stem. A stack of parchments sat beside the bowl.

"This is the sealing of your oath. This parchment has everything on it we talked about. All you must do is sign it in blood." She poured some lamb blood from the pitcher into the bowl. "Here you are." She handed the parchment and the rose to Rahab.

She took a deep breath. This was her life, and she was signing it away.

"Where's my daughter?" Rahab heard an angry voice, her father's voice.

Yassib must have told them he'd set her free of the courtyard to return home. Since she wasn't yet home, her father had come looking for her. She *must* get this signed in time. Not even her father could overturn this pact. If she didn't sign quickly, she'd still be forced to marry Yassib.

Turning her attention to the parchment, she began to carefully scrawl out her name. It was a painfully slow process.

"I said, 'where's my daughter!'" His voice was getting closer. Only a few more letters!

"H-A-" She continued to scrawl as quickly as she could.

"There you are! What do you think you're doing?" Her father screamed in her face. He grabbed her by the collar of her robe, his hand raised to strike her in the face. "You dare go against my wishes?"

She shrank back. "Father, Astarte demanded it of me. She sent me a dream. You have always wanted your children to have a vision from Astarte!"

"You lie, child! Astarte won't speak to the likes of *you*! *You*, not even good enough to be considered a pile of dung. You, who only deserves this." He again raised his hand to strike her.

"I'll thank you for unhanding her," the woman said. "She's the property of Astarte. She signed herself a servant of Astarte in blood just now." She held up the parchment, which contained only half of her last letter, but was good enough to be called signed.

Rahab's father angrily threw her on the floor like a piece of discarded trash. She'd never seen him that mad. Not at her.

"Do you hate me *this* much? So much you'd do this *thing*—" he spat out the word— "without any regard for your family! How am I supposed to return the dowry? My word is broken. My good name is ruined! My business is ruined! Without my business, I can't provide for my family! All. Because. Of. You! I never want to see you again! Never! The day I do is the day you'll die!" He spat on the floor near her, turned on his heel, and angrily stormed away from the daughter he'd disowned.

Rahab crumbled onto the floor and wept. He was right. She'd expected that he'd be angry over her running off like she had, which she had assumed he'd see as rebellion. She hadn't considered her father's good name. She hadn't thought about the dowry her father had already spent on supplies for his meager fish market. She hadn't thought about anything, anyone, but herself and her need to be free of the coming marriage to Yassib. Maybe she should've just gone through with the marriage. Gone through with it and died at Yassib's hand. That would have been better than living a life wishing she were dead. *I* should *be dead. I deserve to die. I am a horrible person, a selfish person, a monster. Forgive me, Astarte, for being a monster.*

"Come, child." A tender hand lay upon her shoulder. She looked up to see her second guide standing behind her.

"Don't offer me compassion. I don't deserve it."

"Let's get you to your dorm. You'll feel better after you're settled, and you get to know the other girls."

Swaying in a seductive way, the way of a prostitute, she led Rahab to her room. *It has become such a habit with these women that they don't even notice they're doing that.* Will that be me one day? Please, Astarte, don't let that be me. I want to get out of here when I've served the time of my pact and lead a normal life, a good life, a life without the stamp of a prostitute.

Chapter 3

The door to her dorm was made of shiny Cyprus, the color of honey. Soothing, welcoming. Rahab ran her fingers over the wood. Smooth and cool. The heavy door creaked on its hinges. *This is much better than the curtains we use to divide rooms at home.* The sweet fragrance of incense filled the room. Excited voices quieted as Rahab and her guide entered the room.

"This is Rahab. Now, I'll let you girls get to know each other." Backing out, her guide closed the door softly.

Instantly, many of the girls were on her, like ants on a drop of honey, asking question after question. All the girls but one. She sat by herself on a pallet huddled in the corner of the room.

"Don't worry about her," a tall, skinny girl with long matted locks and large eyes said. "She's been like that since she got here three days ago. No one can get her to join us for games or to even talk. Don't worry yourself with her. No one else does."

I'm going to make friends with that girl, and then I'm going to help her shine like a dewdrop on the most beautiful rose on a bright, cloudless morning. Everyone will be sorry for treating her like trash.

Rahab looked around the large room. The ceilings were high and vaulted. The walls were Cyprus, like the door, and sanded down to a smooth shine. On the walls hung rosettes, much like those hanging in the temple lobby. There were two windows on the south wall, a lamp on either side of each. Along the walls were pallets, some messy like their occupants had just awoken, and some done up nicely. The floor was smooth rock, and a multi-colored rug with all the colors of the rainbow covered the center of the floor.

"We start training in the morning!" Excitement oozed out of the pores of a short, chunky girl with short curls that were left down in swirls like the whirlpool Rahab had seen six years ago on the southern end of the Jordan River. *Times were better then. Father wasn't so gruff, and mother was happy, almost.*

"Training?" Rahab was completely confused.

"Yes, silly," chirped a girl with light brown, almost green eyes with her hair up in braided locks like most girls in Jericho. "Training."

Rahab stared at her blankly.

"Training to become a temple prostitute, silly!" The girl haughtily tossed her hair behind her and then turned and walked to her pallet, where she sat down and stared off into space.

"You'll have to excuse Ira," said the girl with matted hair. "She comes from a very rich family, and it shows. She's very snobbish. She joined up to bring honor to her family, which I think is silly. Gina," she pointed at the green-eyed girl, "is here for pretty much the same reason, except her family is poor—her family even lives in the poor district of Jericho, as near the outer wall as you can get—and we all know how becoming a temple prostitute brings Astarte's honor on your family and promises prosperity too."

"What about you?"

The girl with the matted hair smiled shyly at her. "The truth?"

"Yes. The whole truth." Rahab shook her head in bewilderment. *Why lie?*

The girl took a deep breath and peered around her like she had a big secret that she didn't want anyone else to know. "I'm an orphan. No mother. No father. Father just died about a month ago. I had no way to support myself. I ran out of food really fast. I thought coming here would get me free food and shelter. Pretty smart, huh?" She elbowed Rahab and smiled expectantly.

Rahab shook her head in shock. "Yeah. What's your name?"

"Orb. My mom named me in honor of my Great Uncle Corbis. Everyone called him Orbie. Thankfully, they just gave me part of his name." She laughed.

"So, um, tell me about this training thing?" Rahab was half curious and half dreading the answer.

"Oh! I'm sorry!" She cupped her hand over her mouth and began to whisper loudly. Rahab was sure everyone could hear her. Everything about Orb was loud. "I'm not really sure *what* it's about. It's kind of mysterious. Apparently, for us to become a temple prostitute, we have to learn the ins and outs of it. Who knows? Maybe it'll be fun!"

Inching away from Orb, who talked very fast and didn't seem to run out of things to say, Rahab moved toward the shy girl in the corner. "Hey. So, I learned all that I could about all the other girls. What's your name?"

The girl turned her back to Rahab and began to weep.

"She does that a lot," Orb announced.

"Let me guess, your parents wanted you to come here, and you obeyed out of respect. You're very respectful and therefore, didn't want to tell them you didn't want to come."

The girl jerked toward Rahab. "How did you know? How *could* you know?"

Rahab smiled. "I didn't. I just guessed. Most of it was pretty easy to guess from your behavior. The rest? I just filled in the blanks. I don't really want to be here either. The difference between you and me is that my parents *don't* want me here."

The shy girl stared at her, a look of confusion on her face.

Rahab sighed. *How did I get into this? How do I get out?* "Suffice it to say that I was forced into it by circumstances."

The shy girl shook her head, her tight, frizzy, kinky curls bobbing with each nod. She still looked confused.

"As you probably already know, I'm Rahab."

"Star."

"Very nice name. I like it. After Astarte, I assume?"

Star again nodded her head.

"And, Star, why are you here?"

"My parents are very religious. They wanted to dedicate their first daughter, after the one sacrificed to Astarte, of course."

"Of course," Rahab said, trying to fill the dead spot. *I'm never having children. I could never murder my first child in the name of sacrifice. I know Astarte, who could never ask us to do evil, requires it, but it still seems so cruel!*

"Anyway, I'm the oldest, so."

"So, you are the one who gets to do the honors."

Star sighed. "I guess you could put it that way."

I'm going to make this girl my friend!

One of the women in a see-through robe came into the room with towels and rags. "Bath time," she sang.

The girls all looked at each other in confusion, and then shrugged their shoulders.

"Who am I to complain," chirped Orb. "Free baths!"

Everyone giggled and followed their guide to a large heated spring that was conveniently located inside its own room. The room was fogged with steam, making it difficult to see very far. The spring was large enough to comfortably fit all of the girls at once and to still have room to spare. It was surrounded with smooth, shiny, flat stones in a vast array of different colors. The inside of the spring was colored much the same as the floor surrounding it. *Wow! These people spare no expense!* Rahab knew Astarte could provide anything the temple might need or want, but this was amazing.

Removing their clothes, they quickly bathed in the warm water and climbed out to dry off. After they dressed in the clean clothes their guide provided, a thick sheath of many thin robes, the top one violet in color, their guide and four other guides brushed out the girls' hair and put it up in braids. Next, they were perfumed with beautifully scented incense and sent back to their dorm.

What does tomorrow hold? Training. Rahab was very nervous. Nervous to the point of being terrified, nervous to the point of nausea. She hated surprises. Though she lay on a warm, very comfortable pallet, Rahab knew she'd never get any sleep.

Tomorrow.

Chapter 4

"Time to arise, ladies. You start your training today." Rahab thought she was dreaming when her guide from the day before spoke from the doorway. "Today is the most important day of the rest of your life. Now arise. Dress quickly."

"Rahab! Wake up!" Orb sang as she enthusiastically shook Rahab from her slumber. "Today is training!"

"Mmm." Rahab felt like she hadn't slept in days. She sat on the edge of her pallet in a daze. Running her hands over her hair, she could feel that some of her braids had already started to work itself loose. *Already? They were just braided yesterday.* She sighed in defeat.

Mmm! I smell breakfast. Scents of fried pork, poached eggs, and frying potatoes wafted into the girls' living quarters.

With a new determination, Rahab was dressed and joined the other girls congregated around the closed door. When their guide returned, she led them to their morning meal.

With full bellies and happy hearts, the girls were ready to tackle the day.

"Follow me." *These people are always so… right to business.* After quietly leading the girls through a seemingly endless maze, the woman spoke again, "Please take a seat.

"Astarte once went to the underworld on a mission of love. Her lover, Tammuz, had died, and she journeyed below to rescue her beloved. On her way, she came up against the gates of the underworld. She knocked, demanding that they be opened. Being the goddess of all, she got her wish under certain circumstances. She had to remove one of her seven veil-like robes, each one a different color of the Chakras and the rainbow before the gatekeeper would allow her through his gate."

That explains these silly robes they had us dress in. Astarte's clothing was made up of seven layers of robes, each a different color, each see-through when standing alone, but a completely modest robe when worn in layers, one over the other.

"Upon passing through the seventh gate, Astarte was naked, her black skin revealed in all its glory. The goddess was only allowed to enter the Underworld when she was stripped of her powers, completely naked and defenseless. You will take that same journey through similar gates during your training."

Rahab peered down at her clothing. The robes were held together with a sash. She wore ornate sandals decorated with gems and braided leather. Each girl was given a matching ruby bracelet and anklet and a rainbow-colored necklace holding seven gems, each a different color of the rainbow. Teardrop shaped earrings hung from their ears. They were given breast cups to wear, something she had never seen. They were made of palm leaves, held together by silk, and lifted one's breast in a rather awkward position. Lastly, they were given a gold diadem to set upon their head, its shape like that of a thousand petals.

Rahab looked up, suddenly aware that everything had become eerily quiet around her. Ahead of her, where her guide had been standing and effectively blocking her view, was a door covered in jewels from top to bottom, each one shining and glittering, each trying to outdo the rest. The jewels were arranged in a rainbow, each portion of the door covered with a different color making up all the colors of the rainbow from violet at the top, then indigo, blue, green, yellow, orange, and red. It was truly amazing. Breathtaking. The prettiest thing Rahab had ever seen.

"How do we get in?" The guide asked.

Why is she asking us? Doesn't she know?

Star spoke up, quietly, yet loud enough to be heard. Everyone hushed and stared in awe. Star never spoke. They held their breath so they could hear what she had to say. "You knock."

Oh! The story! Knock.

No one moved. Rahab looked around at everyone, apparently frozen in place. She slowly stood, drawing everyone's attention and walked up to the door. For the first time, she noticed it had no handle, no way to get in. Out of curiosity, she pushed it. She pushed hard. It didn't budge. *Strange.* She tentatively knocked. Almost immediately, the heavy door swung open so all who would enter could.

Rahab timidly pushed the door open. There was no one in the room. *Who opened the door?* The room was white. Too white. On the walls hung colorful paintings of Astarte in her different forms. The pictures seemed to flow, telling a story Rahab didn't know. She searched the panels, trying to decipher their meaning.

"This is your resting place for now. You'll be here until after you have eaten your lunch, then we'll proceed to the first gate. Mingle. Relax. Do as you wish. Just don't leave." Their guide turned and quietly closed the door behind her.

Rahab wondered what time it was. She had no way of knowing. Her stomach said it was close to lunchtime. She'd go with her stomach.

After lunch, the girls anxiously awaited the return of their guide.

Rahab and Star were off alone in a corner. They weren't talking. They were just sitting together away from the mingling that neither one really wanted to be a part of.

Ira was trying to use the glare off the white wall to fix her hair in the reflection. Gina was staring at the floor, her beautiful brown eyes filled with tears that threatened to spill over. Rahab felt for her. She knew how she felt.

Why did I do this? What did I get myself into? *Please, Astarte, help my father's business to prosper so he can care for my family. Please don't punish my family for my selfishness. Why was I so selfish? And then to leave the little ones with no one to care for them. Selfish.*

"Before we can proceed, you must learn to smell like a goddess." Their guide had returned. *How did she get in?* Rahab hadn't heard her knock. "This scent is only allowed on temple prostitutes and only during your years at the temple. You will be expected to make your own, so listen carefully. You will combine one-part mixed cereal grains, two parts of the resin from acacia, one-half part vine leaves, one half part date palm leaves, a few drops of the oil from frankincense, and one-part frankincense. Any questions?"

They sure don't ask a lot. Rahab's mind was reeling with sarcastic remarks.

"During your training, the scent will be provided for you." Three ladies came in and applied a little of the

36

scent to each girl. *Sure doesn't take much.* Rahab immediately recognized the smell as the one the guides around the temple wore. *But it's only for temple prostitutes? They must be temple prostitutes, too! Maybe to a higher class of men?*

"Since there are no questions, let's move on."

The woman motioned them toward the second door in the room. This one was covered in solid violet jewels. Rahab wondered what kind of gem they had used.

"Upon entering this first gate, you will surrender the first layer of your robes, the violet one, and your belt and sandals. Astarte did this as she passed through the first gate. This pictures the fact that you are relinquishing your will. You will now is to follow Astarte, to do as she wills and only as she wills. Give up your will. Sacrifice it to Astarte."

Each of the girls removed their sandals and robe as they whispered among themselves. Rahab felt a little more self-conscious. A little less clothed. She still had enough on to cover her, but she subconsciously felt revealed.

Stepping through the door, Rahab saw the floor was made up of raked sand. *Sand?* It was raked into flowing circular patterns. Five sets of stones lay in different places around the room. Each set held seven smooth stones of differing sizes and colors arranged in a small wheel shape. *What?*

There was another guide awaiting them in the new room. "The next thing you need to know is The Spell. It is used to transform your energy so your mind and body can be balanced so you can more fully serve Astarte."

Their guide told them each to choose a set of stones and sit beside it. "There are seven doors to your energy, your life-force. These doors are similar to the gates to the underworld. Each one of the doors maintains a different part of your health. They must stay balanced and aligned; otherwise, your physical, mental, emotional, and spiritual health will be compromised."

Rahab picked up a red stone. Now that she was able to examine it up close, she realized they were not stones at all, but crystals. It was smooth and cool. Its oval shape lay perfect in her hand. The other six stones were orange, yellow, green, blue, indigo, and violet. *Astarte must really like rainbows.*

Each of the girls carefully followed the precise instruction given to them as more guides entered the room. *The help.* Cleansing the crystals was pretty basic. They were provided with a basin of warm soapy water and a soft, velvety rag. She carefully wet and scrubbed each stone and dried them with a second rag. Next, the girls were told to lie upon their backs. They were quickly able to get comfortable in the warm sand.

Rahab was surprised to find that the rainbow of crystals had to be laid on her body in a certain order. The red crystal, which balances one's sense of reality, physical energy, motivation, and practicality, was placed on the sand between her legs. The orange crystal, which balances creativity and the ability to feel enjoyment, was placed below her navel. The yellow one was set on her diaphragm to help clear her mind, raise self-confidence, and balance creativity. The green crystal, she was told, would bring balance, calm, and direction in one's life. This was placed gently on her chest. Blue, the bringer of peace and the ability to communicate with ease was set on her throat in a whisper of movement. The indigo crystal was set just above her eyes and would give her understanding, clarity of thought, and increased intuition and memory. The last crystal, the violet one, was set on the sand at the top of Rahab's head. She shivered as the stone passed through a bit of her hair. She was told that this crystal would integrate every aspect of her health.

After lying relaxed in the quiet stillness with the stones on her for many minutes, Rahab did feel better, more at peace with herself. They again cleansed the stones, but this time, they were instructed on how to store them in a safe place.

"The best thing to do is to keep them in a glass pitcher in a sunny window. These stones are for you to keep. Use them regularly. Your service to Astarte depends on you being in balance."

As the days passed, Rahab quickly became bored with the training. At the second gate, she had to give up her next robe and her bracelet and anklet, thus relinquishing her ego. Gate number three was a relinquishing of her mind.

She was more and more self-conscious about her lack of clothing as she passed through each gate. One week between gates wasn't nearly enough time.

Gate four, the green gate, claimed her breast cups. *Thank you, Astarte! Who invented those things anyway? So uncomfortable!* This gate also claimed her power over her ability to give or receive the pleasures of sex without Astarte's approval. At the fifth gate, Rahab was asked to give up her illumination—*What illumination? I'm not smart enough for that*—and her rainbow necklace. The sixth gate, a beautiful orange color, claimed her earrings and any claim to magic she or her family might hold. *No loss there.*

By now, she was down to one very see-through red robe. On the other side of the next gate, gate seven, she'd be completely naked. At gate seven, she was forced to surrender her golden diadem and her last bit of clothing. Standing before her friends completely naked was embarrassing enough, but the last gate led them into a room occupied by seven naked men. Rahab felt her face flush brightly, not only at what she saw but also at the fact that she was also naked. She wished for a place to hide but could find none.

"In this room," their guide said, "the male temple prostitutes will help you on your next step of the journey." *Male prostitutes? I didn't even* know *there* were *male temple prostitutes!* "The next step is to learn not to be shy around men and to be able to freely give yourself to any man for any pleasure he wishes. These men will help you."

Men? Help? Not be shy? Able to freely give? Rahab knew what was expected of her, but she wholeheartedly wished it wasn't so. If only she could go home. If only she could see her family one more time. If only. *If only. I did this to myself. My selfish self. I deserve every last bit of what I get. Here or anywhere.* Yassib had already stolen her virginity. What else could they take? *Help me, Astarte.* She wasn't sure Astarte would even answer. She was beginning to wonder if Astarte really cared. If she was even really there at all.

Regardless, I'm stuck here now. Time to put on a pretty face and endure.

Chapter 5

The pain was fierce, but the priestesses were right. It did ease up with time, but the embarrassment. Rahab had spent one long, grueling week on the other side of gate seven, but regardless of the length of time, she would never get used to flaunting her naked body.

Why did I... how could I have lowered myself to such a degrading level?

Rahab reminded herself that she'd chosen the temple over Yassib, a much worse fate. She set a new resolution. She would survive her seven years. No, she would do more than survive, she would flourish. She would watch. She would learn. As soon as she could, she'd free herself from this slavery. *Three weeks down, not including training. I can do this. At least I can try.*

Rahab shuffled along, head down, hugging herself, toward the other girls who were huddled in a loose circle.

Orb visibly shuddered. "I saw it today. The statue."

The other girls stared at her blankly, not understanding what she was trying to say.

"*The* statue," Orb repeated.

They still didn't understand.

Orb lowered her voice even further, so low that Rahab could barely hear her. "The idol they use to burn the firstborn babies alive as a sacrifice to Astarte!"

The girls looked at her in understanding, a look of disgust upon many of their faces.

"It's gold and a little taller than a normal man. Its arms are out, cupped where they place the baby. The arms allow the baby to roll down into the belly of the idol, which must have a very hot fire burning inside. The bottom half of the idol is some other type of metal—iron, I think. It was just barely glowing red."

"How do you know about how the babies are held and how they roll down into the idol?" Gina looked like she sincerely wanted to know.

Orb shuddered again. She swallowed hard and took a deep, shaky breath, her eyes brimming in tears. She tried to blink them back but to no avail.

"I saw it. I saw them sacrifice a baby." Her tears spilled over. "The baby screamed for what seemed like forever. Horrible, high pitched screams of agony." She tried to wipe her tears away as more came. "And to think we'll have to. To sacrifice. Our firstborn. Like. That." A ragged breath escaped her. "How can we *not* get pregnant? Our *job* will have most of us pregnant by the end of the month. If we're not already. Then we'll have to do this awful thing!"

Rahab reached out and pulled her in a tight embrace, holding her until she had finished crying. No words were said. No words were needed.

Gina's eyes brightened. "I remember hearing someone talking about how to keep from getting pregnant! It was with plants. Let me think." She mulled over it then sighed in defeat.

"Think hard." Rahab gently laid her hand on Gina's shoulder. "For all of us."

Rahab loved flowers, but she didn't know of any that prevented pregnancy. "I'll name some plants. It's probably one that's poisonous, but just enough to cause a miscarriage and not enough to kill you or make you too sick. Acacia Gum? Queens Anne's Lace? Silphium?"

Gina's eyes lit up again. "Silphium! It was Silphium!"

The tiny group of girls sighed simultaneously, relief flooding over them.

"It may be hard to find enough for all of us to use for very long." Rahab shook her head and bit her bottom lip.

Silphium was highly sought after. It was difficult to find, but Rahab knew where to look. Places that weren't well known. She hoped there'd be enough.

Rahab had smelled perfumes and eaten seasonings made from the essence of Silphium. She loved the taste of the stalk and the way the leaves made a dish stand out when used as a garnish. Silphium could be used to heal any number of diseases and infections. The apple lady claimed that it had healed her of dysentery. Her neighbor used it in a poultice when a serpent bit her son last autumn. It took all the poison out and saved the boy's life. Now, on top of all the other great things she knew about Silphium, it was also a form of birth control.

Star's posture slumped as she turned away from the others and slowly walked toward a stone bench. Rahab followed her. She placed her hand on her shoulder. "Star, what's wrong?"

"I—I can't use the Silphium."

"Why? It's our only hope of keeping ourselves from getting pregnant."

"I can't use it because it's wrong to stop pregnancy. My other god wouldn't approve of killing an innocent baby." Star looked flushed. "Even in the womb."

"God? You serve more than just Astarte?"

"I also serve the God of Israel. My father learned of Him on his last journey into the wilderness to trade for furs." Star suddenly looked scared. "You can't tell anyone! Especially anyone here!"

"Your secret's safe with me." Rahab drew an X on her lips. "But you really should consult with your gods on this birth control thing. Besides, it's not killing a baby. When you start using it, there won't be a baby in your womb. It's a preventative, and you don't want to watch and hear your first baby die."

Star lowered her eyes, tears flowing. "You don't understand."

What was there to understand? Rahab stared at Star, confused.

Star's whole body began to quiver. "I'm pretty sure I'm already pregnant." She looked up at Rahab—a plea for help in her eyes. "My menses is two weeks late."

Rahab didn't know what to say, so she simply gathered Star into her arms. Her friend wilted against her and began to cry in big, mournful sobs, sobs of hopelessness and despair.

As the weeks passed, Rahab watched Star grew larger and larger with child and fall deeper into depression. Why didn't she just take the Silphium and end the pregnancy? Surely her god didn't intend on allowing her baby to be sacrificed.

Soon after the Silphium discovery, Rahab learned that Queen Anne's Lace was also not only a contraceptive but that it also caused an early miscarriage. It might not have been effective with how far along Star was, but it would've been worth a try.

Star seemed to grow more distant as she drew closer to the time the baby was to come. She refused to hold even a small conversation. She even refused to make eye contact. She walked wide berths around people to keep as much distance between them and herself as she could.

At first, Rahab thought it was due to the fact that she'd have to sacrifice her baby, but she soon began to see other oddities, changes that she couldn't figure out. Star avoided knives and ropes like the plague. She no longer liked to be alone. Even though she was around people more, she sat in a corner away from everyone else. She cried a lot and often got a wild, scared look on her face. Rahab tried to ask her what was wrong. She offered to listen.

"That's what best friends are for, right?"

Star didn't budge. She wouldn't talk about the horrible torment she appeared to be going through.

Rahab worried constantly about her dear friend. *If only she would talk to me.*

The day finally came for Star to have her baby. Such a joyful time, such a joyful experience. Only it wasn't joyful for Star. She wept all the way through the labor, and not just from the contractions. She was bent over with pains. The strained look on her face was from more than just the labor. *If only she would just talk to me!*

"Rahab!" Star called out. "I need you!"

Rahab was in the room trying to stay out of the way of the priestesses assisting in the birth. When Star cried her name, Rahab rushed to the pallet and clasped her friend's outstretched hands in hers. Rahab could feel that Star was shaking uncontrollably.

"It won't be long now," the priestess that served the temple as the midwife said. "You'll start to feel the urge to push, Star. Just listen to your body. Push when you feel the need, and this baby will just pop right out."

Star pushed and pushed. Finally, Rahab saw a head starting to peek out. "The baby is coming!" She squeezed Star's hand. "Keep pushing!"

A few moments later, Rahab heard a cry. The cry of the baby.

"It's a girl," the midwife priestess said matter-of-factly, no emotion in her voice.

"She's beautiful!" Rahab gasped. "Oh, Star! You did a great job."

But Star wasn't listening. She was crying into her pillow.

"Star?" Rahab laid a hand on her friend's shoulder. "What's wrong, Honey?"

She continued to cry, great gut-wrenching sobs.

Rahab thought it was the doom of the impending sacrifice that was bothering her. The priestesses had already left, so they were no help. Most mothers would be cuddling their child, most mothers would be smothering their baby in kisses, but Star refused to even look at her child. When she ran out of tears, she turned her face to the wall.

Where's her joy? Why's she acting like this? Talk to me, Star! Just talk to me!

Rahab took the baby, cleaned her, and wrapped her. Star refused to nurse her daughter, so Rahab took her away in search of goat's milk, praying it would be enough.

For the next two weeks, Rahab cared for the baby. She tried to stay detached, tried to not fall in love. If she fell in love, she'd bear such great pain when the sacrifice came. But it was of no use. She fell in love. How could she not? The baby was so beautiful. So perfect.

Star refused to see the baby and even refused to give her a name.

"It's kind of weird calling her 'Baby' all the time, Star."

Star rolled over on her pallet, her tearful face toward the wall. Great sobs escaped her.

Rahab sighed loudly enough for Star to hear. "If you don't name her soon, then I will." Rahab stared hard at Star's back. "Fine." She was decisive and firm. "I'll name her Lily Rose."

She stared at Star's back once more. No response.

With a sigh, Rahab turned to shuffle out with Lily Rose in her arms.

"That's a beautiful name." Star's voice was so low that Rahab barely heard it. "A name I'd expect from you. A name inspired by your wonderful love of beautiful flowers."

Rahab held her breath, not daring to make a sound lest the magic that was happening in that room stop. As far as Rahab knew, Star hadn't spoken since Lily was born.

Star took a deep breath, perhaps to speak again, and stopped.

Please keep talking.

Rahab walked slowly over to Star's bed and lowered herself onto the edge. She sat there. Hoping against all hope.

"I don't know what to do." Star turned her face into Rahab's leg and started to sob. "I just don't know what to do. The thoughts. They just come out of nowhere. I see what I *want* to do. Only. I don't *want* to do it. I don't want to kill myself. I don't want to kill my baby, but the thoughts won't stop! If you have her, she's safe." Her words spilled out, coming between gasps. "What kind of mother has thoughts of killing her own child? *This* kind. This miserable, unworthy kind.

Unworthy of life. Unworthy of anything. I wish I could just die. Then the baby would truly be safe." Rahab sat silently stroking her friend's matted hair, hoping she had more to say. "Promise me you'll keep her," Star whispered. "That you'll keep her safe. Safe from me. Safe from everything. Keep her safe, Rahab."

Rahab looked down at Lily, peacefully sleeping in her arms, oblivious to what was transpiring. "I promise."

A new resolution took hold of Rahab. She *would* keep Lily safe. Whatever the cost.

With that, the magic was broken. Star rolled away and would speak no further.

As the months dragged by, Star grew worse. She started talking to herself, hiding in corners from imaginary monsters, and sobbing uncontrollably. She refused to groom herself. Even the simple task of brushing her hair continued to be beyond her. Rahab went to visit her often, taking Lily with her every time. Due to Star's worsening condition, she couldn't risk getting Lily too close. Still, Star refused to touch or hold her baby.

"Keep. Her. Safe." Star shivered, huddled in one of her favorite corners. She hadn't spoken since their last conversation. "They'll get her! Don't let them get her!"

"Who?" Rahab grew even more concerned.

"The priestesses. Don't let them get her! She's almost a year old. The deadline to sacrifice your baby. The oldest they can possibly be. Don't let them get her!"

Just then, like clockwork, two priestesses walked into the room. They stood in the doorway, peering into the darkness. Their long see-through robes rustled in the light breeze. Their ornate bracelets, large earrings, gem-lined tiaras, and gaudy necklaces shimmered in the bright sunshine.

"Astarte demands a sacrifice," said one of the priestesses.

"No!" Star leaped to her feet from the corner where she was cowering and rushed toward them in a frenzy, arms flailing. "No!" Then suddenly she shrank back and began muttering to herself once again.

One of the priestesses reached for Lily. Rahab didn't know what to do. She stood there in shock. Surely it was too early. Surely Lily wasn't old enough to be sacrificed.

Star leaped between Lily in Rahab's arms and the priestess. As the other priestess tried to take Lily from Rahab, Star pounced on her, biting her arm and tearing at her with unclipped fingernails. The second priestess quickly came to the other's aid, prying Star off her, but not before receiving a few battle wounds of her own. They left quickly without looking back.

The next day, Rahab walked up on a group of girls whispering amongst themselves.

"Have you heard?" Gina asked in a low voice. "Star went crazy on some of the priestesses when they came to get her baby!"

"They're not going to make her sacrifice the baby," Orb confided in an equally low voice. "I heard the priestesses say that, since Star is full of demons, the baby is a tainted sacrifice."

"Do you want to know what I think?" Another girl spoke up. "I think they're just scared to go in and face her again."

"They tried everything to expel her demons," Orb said. "They tied her down and did the spell on her and everything. They thought that maybe getting her energies back in balance would fix her problems, but we all know that didn't work."

Tainted sacrifice? Rahab had never heard of such a thing, but she supposed it was possible. *Not going to make her sacrifice the baby?* Rahab's heart leaped in her chest. Could it be true? Could Lily truly be safe? Or was it just more temple gossip? She had to tell Star!

Rahab rushed toward Star's room. In the doorway, she paused. A horrible sense of foreboding came upon her. Something had happened. Something bad. She started forward again. Slowly, taking a shaky, deep breath, she entered Star's room to let her eyes adjust to the dimness. Star was in her usual corner, but she was crumpled in a heap among broken pottery.

"Star?" Rahab set Lily on Star's pallet and rushed to Star's side. Taking her by the shoulder, she gently shook it. "Star?" She shook her harder, but there still was no response.

Rahab's breath caught in her throat. Her chest grew tight. Tears sprung into her eyes. She pulled Star out of the weird heap and laid her on her back. Star was covered in blood. Rahab started to weep. There was a long, deep slice on Star's wrist. She had taken her life.

When Rahab stood up, a piece of parchment on the small dining table caught her eye. She wiped her tears and reached for it.

"Rahab," the parchment read in hurried, sloppy scrawl—not the once beautiful handwriting of her friend, "I have to go now. My time has come. I can't live like this any longer. I know the baby will be safe with you. Keep her safe. She's yours now. Keep her safe. Star."

Rahab returned to Lily, picking her up from the pallet and looked over at Star again. Lily would never remember her real mother. Her beautiful, deeply caring, wonderful mother. She would never have that blessing. Rahab determined that *she* would be the best mother any child could have, the mother Lily deserved. And she would tell Lily all about her real mother. How wonderful she was. She'd build memories for her.

Rahab took a deep breath. In one day, she had lost her best friend and gained a child, a child she loved dearly. A child the priestesses might try to steal from her in the name of sacrifice. She wouldn't let that happen. She would not. She had made a solemn promise. A promise she *would* keep. She would protect her beautiful Lily Rose. Whatever the cost.

Chapter 6

Beautiful, beautiful Lily Rose. Rahab stroked the long dark locks of her child, no longer a baby. *Six years old. I can't believe she's already six years old!* Lily had just had another birthday, another birthday devoid of friends. No one wanted to be friends with the daughter of a prostitute. No parent would allow it, but Lily didn't seem to mind.

During the day, while Rahab serviced Astarte, Lily attended a school run by priestesses within the temple walls. A school created for children like Lily, children born as a result of holy prostitution. There weren't any children Lily's age since many of the mothers continued to worship Astarte by sacrificing more than just their first baby, and since the discovery of Silphium had been shared temple wide.

Lily stirred, ever so slightly. Rahab held her breath hoping she had not awakened her. Lily nestled back into her covers and fell back into a deep slumber with a soft sigh.

How would she be able to care for Lily after her slavery to Astarte, as she had become fond of calling it, finished in less than a week? She had quite a bit set back. All the jewelry she'd owned during her years would still be hers when she left. Her small fortune wouldn't last forever, though. And she'd need to purchase a home, the perfect home to raise Lily.

Rahab's greatest worry was how to keep Lily from following in her footsteps. How could she show her a life without prostitution, a life of purity? Lily had been raised for so long in an environment that condoned it. Rahab vowed she'd raise Lily to be a pure, proper lady.

Rahab heard a noise and turned her head toward the door to her chamber.

"Can I come in?" Orb asked meekly. *Meek? That's not like her.*

Rahab looked tenderly down at Lily again before pushing herself up from the pallet. She moved silently toward the door and stepped outside into the starlight. "What's wrong?"

Orb reached out and held both of Rahab's hands. She stared at the ground and then finally looked up into Rahab's eyes. "I'm staying."

Rahab gasped. "Staying? Why?"

"I have to. I have no other place to go. I have no family, no ties, no bonds. There's nothing else I *can* do. I have to stay."

Rahab understood. She didn't have anywhere to go either. Her father had disowned her, and her mother would not be allowed to communicate with her or help her along. That's why she was so happy for the jewels she was leaving with. Jewels to buy a home for her and Lily.

Now it was her turn to stare at the ground. "You could come with Lily and me."

"I can't. I've already signed a new contract." Orb slowly shook her head, a sob catching in her throat. "Anyway, I just wanted to let you know." She took a deep breath. "I'm going to miss you and Lily both so much. Please take care of yourselves."

Orb turned and walked briskly away.

Rahab blinked back tears. Staying? Why? She could've found a way out like Rahab did. Orb didn't have to stay. She could come with her and Lily.

"Mama?" Lily called from her pallet.

"I'm right here, Honey." Rahab looked after Orb for just a moment longer before turning to go inside and settling beside Lily.

"Mama, I'm scared." Lily sat on the edge of the pallet clutching her rag doll. She'd had that doll since she was a toddler. The priestess Tisha, Lily's favorite, had made it for her. It was stained and tattered, yet Lily still loved it more than anything else in her little world, everything, that is, except her mother.

Rahab pulled Lily into her arms. She knew what scared Lily. It was the same every night. Nightmares. Horrible dreams of being thrown into the furnace, sacrificed to Asarte. Ever since the priestesses had taught the children about the obligation—the blessing of every mother to sacrifice their first baby to Astarte—Lily had grown more and more scared that the priestesses would make Rahab sacrifice her.

"Don't worry, Honey. They won't make me sacrifice you. Your mother made sure that would never happen. She loved you so very much."

Lily pushed away just enough to look up at Rahab. "Why'd she have to go away? Why'd she leave me?"

Rahab had answered so many questions about Star lately. She was very glad that Lily wanted to know more about her mother. She hoped she'd never stop asking questions. At the same time, she hoped she'd never ask questions that would be too hard to answer, questions that would tell exactly what happened to her mother and why. If it came to that, Rahab would tell the truth. All of it. But not until Lily was older, much older, old enough to understand and accept it for what it was, a saga of true love.

"She went away to keep you safe. She died as a sacrifice for you."

"Like how babies are sacrificed to Astarte?"

"Kind of like that." Rahab ran her fingers through Lily's soft hair. "She made the choice to die so that you could be safe."

She nestled her face into Lily's hair. Rahab loved her smell. She drew Lily against her breast once more and began singing *her* song to her. The song she'd written for Lily when she was a baby and sang to her often.

"The sun is setting in the west.
The birds are nuzzling in their nest.
The smell of flowers in the air.
Not a worry, not a care.
The sound of a breeze on a summer day
Whisking all our cares away.
Like our love that's here to stay,
Love so strong and pure.
Listen to the moon's soft song.
Hear the stars as they sing along.
The crickets chirp their lullabies
The breeze whispers, and it sighs.
So go to sleep now. Rest your head.
Close your eyes upon your bed.
Bask in love both shown and said.
Rest in this love so sure."

By the end of the song, Lily was fast asleep, safely wrapped in her mother's arms. Rahab lowered her onto the pallet and busied herself around her chamber, worrying about the details.

Where would Lily go to school? Would she be accepted? Would the temple send Rahab out naked or give her clothing? How would she go about getting herself set up and established in a brand new world? A brand new world. It was scary.

As Rahab drifted off to sleep, her last thought was of Yassib. Would he still be waiting to torment her when she got out? Would he truly be seeking revenge? He had visited her at least once a week, demanding her services, forcing her into painful and embarrassing positions, and each week he promised to make her pay for the missed wedding all those years ago. Would he really follow through, or were they empty threats?

The next morning greeted Rahab with bright, cheerful sunshine pouring through her windows. The birds were singing. A soft breeze blew through the window by her pallet, rustling her out of her sleep, wafting the smell of fresh flowers into her room.

Turning onto her back, she stretched way above her head, arching her spine like a newborn baby, trying to force the sleep from her joints. Then she rolled up on her elbow, looked over at Lily, and smiled. She was so beautiful. A sleeping angel.

Time to get on with the day. Rolling out of bed, Rahab donned a fresh see-through robe that the temple prostitutes were allowed to wear when not "on duty." Although a little more comfortable, her nakedness was still very easily seen. *I'll never get used to this.* With only two days left, she wouldn't have to for long.

Getting Lily dressed and ready for the day seemed to go by much too fast. Rahab loved her time with Lily. She relished their mornings and evenings, the only hours they had together.

She took her time walking Lily to the temple schoolroom. What will we do when we don't have the temple school to rely on? Who will watch Lily while I'm at work? Will she be accepted at the new school? Rahab kept her thoughts to herself but worried about them incessantly.

Walking through the temple still awed her. It never changed, yet she always found something new. Today was no different. Her thoughts lately leaned more towards how the different things could be utilized in the outside world. Suddenly, the bright shimmering drapes became long, flowing robes. The beautiful golden stars on the wall became dishes, and the potted trees became decorations in a home of her own.

Rahab was barely sixteen years old when she'd signed away seven years of her life, so she knew close to nothing about the outside world. What she had known, she'd forgotten. Her mother had done all the cooking. Even shopping would be hard after seven years of being waited on. Then there was getting a job. How would she find work if she had no skills?

Rahab paused at the fountain that had drawn her in on her first day. She walked up to it, peering into the water. *How will I make it happen?*

"Mama?" Lily tugged on her robe.

Rahab snapped back to the present, sighed and turned to walk her darling treasure the rest of the way to her schoolroom. Sudden doubts engulfed her. How was she going to survive in the world outside the temple walls and care for Lily? Maybe she should just sign up for another seven years of servitude.

Only two more days. What would the days after that bring? How would she ever survive?

The next two days passed the same way that every other day before had passed. The difference was the rising excitement, along with the rising apprehension that was mounting inside Rahab, each warring against the other, making her sway between going and staying. Tossing her back and forth, back and forth, like a boat tossed on a stormy sea. No wonder so many women signed on so many extra times as a temple prostitute. If it wasn't for Lily, she probably would've too, just to stay where everything was familiar.

Move out day. Rahab was glad the temple furnished her with a whole wardrobe of modest outfit for the outside world. Lily, too, was allowed to keep her temple-provided clothing.

Gathering her belongings onto a small cart, she took one last look at her room. She'd lived there for so long that she hated to leave it. It felt like a part of her. She was already beginning to feel homesick for her soft pallet and her favorite seat by the west-facing window.

The trek wasn't long. She was just going down the street to the closest boarding house. The air was muggy, the dust was thick, the streets were loud and crowded, and the mixed smell of horse and sweat hung in the air, but Rahab was on top of the world, her doubts and apprehensions left behind.

Her seven years were over. She was out. She and Lily were finally free. Life was going to be great! She hoped.

She planned to get settled in today and start looking for a home tomorrow. She had a house in mind. She wanted to see if the house on the wall, the house she had drooled over every day of her life before her temple days, was still vacant. She smiled inside. Her dreams were finally beginning to come true. She couldn't wait to get everything rolling. Tomorrow looked promising. Yet tomorrow seemed like a long time away.

Chapter 7

Rahab stood in the dusty street, looking at her new home. The house on top of the city walls that she'd loved since she was a child. What had she ever done that allowed her to see all her dreams come true? She smiled wide. A warm joy flowed through her, filling and overflowing her heart. She was so taken with her new home that she didn't even notice the bustle of the street, the dust that filled her nostrils, the smell of horse and sweat, or the hot sun on her back.

Buying the house had been quick and painless. The people who had owned it had wanted to get rid of it as quickly as possible. They'd been trying to sell it for a number of years, but no one wanted to pay their price. *How could anyone not want this house?* Rahab had plenty of funds to spare between the jewelry she was allowed to keep and the money given to her by the temple. Upon completion of her vow, the temple gave every holy prostitute enough money to get on her feet, for which Rahab was grateful.

Walking through her new home for the first time was the most exciting experience of her life. She had always appreciated the outside of the house. She had drooled over it every time she walked past it. The inside was equally stunning.

Standing at the threshold, she gazed around her in wonder. The walls were made of the same mud bricks as the outside. She walked through the arched front door and into a massive room. The ceiling was high and vaulted, the floor made of the stones used to build the city walls. The room had a number of windows, all rounded, some facing to the east and some to the west. Rahab pictured her and Lily sitting in this room and watching the sun rise and set every day.

The large room had two doors, one leading to a massive kitchen. Rahab was stunned to see that it was completely furnished with a fireplace, hearth, oven, small spring-fed reservoir for keeping food cold, and spring-fed basin for cooking and washing. The other door led to a slightly smaller room that had a staircase off to one side. Walking up the staircase, she noticed a little give in one of the wooden steps. *I'll need to fix that as soon as possible.*

At the top of the staircase was a long hall, open to the lower story on one side and edged with a custom banister with spiraled slats and topped with big wooden balls. The hallway wrapped around the outer wall of the entire lower story room. There were six bedrooms off the hallway, three on each straight stretch, each a decent size. Rahab couldn't imagine ever needing so many rooms. Her family would never come to visit her. Her father had already made his position clear on that.

The large house spread out in every direction, room after room, each more impressive than the last. As she toured her new home, Rahab grew more and more excited. Her excitement and wonder spilled over onto Lily, making her a bustling ball of energy. Rahab grabbed her hands and danced with her in twirls and swirls until they were both out of breath. Then they collapsed onto the cool floor in jubilant laughter.

Moving their belongings into their new home was easy since they didn't have much. *Time to remedy that.*

"Let's go shopping!" Rahab exclaimed.

She knew they should probably save their money, but right now she didn't care. Rahab wanted her house to be beautiful. She'd buy coverings for the windows, real wooden furniture, and hangings for the walls. They also needed some more practical things like dishes and food, and Lily needed clothes that fit her properly. She was growing so fast that she was quickly outgrowing the clothes she had.

"Stay close to me," Rahab instructed Lily as they left the house.

The streets seemed more crowded than normal. Rahab and Lily were bumped and jostled as they moved through the press. They spent all afternoon searching for exactly what they wanted. Rahab found rose-colored satin drapes for the windows, fuzzy, rose-colored area rugs for each main room, and multiple wall hangings. She bought cedar wood couches with gray upholstery and white pillows. She bought cedar beds for the bedrooms and individually colored sheets, pillows, and quilts. The dishes she bought were plain white with a picture of a lily along one edge. Rahab paid for the last of her purchases and sighed, happy and satisfied.

"Let's go, Lily," she said, her voice heavy with the tiredness she felt. She turned, but Lily wasn't with her. "Lily!" She yelled as loudly as she could, but her voice was lost in the tumult of the marketplace. "Lily!"

She searched around her. She jogged up and down the streets, frantic, pushing her way through the crowd. Lily was nowhere. *Astarte, if you're there, help me find her. Let her be safe! Please!*

Rahab rushed from place to place, everywhere they'd been, every vendor they'd visited. She asked each person if they'd seen a little girl wandering about. None of them had. She called out to passing strangers, hoping someone, anyone, had seen Lily. No one seemed to hear her.

"Lily!" Tears stung Rahab's eyes. *Where is my baby girl?*

At the first vendor they'd visited together, the proprietor told Rahab he'd seen a little girl with dark braids wandering near the alley next to his shop.

Rahab rushed toward the alley, tripping over strangers' feet, and nearly falling several times. "Lily!" she shouted. "Lily!"

Rounding the corner into the alleyway, Rahab slowed her pace. There, tucked in a corner, huddled a little girl. Rahab nearly wept in relief.

"Lily!" She rushed toward her. Lily didn't stir. *Let her be okay.*

Rahab reached Lily and gathered her daughter into her arms. Lily rubbed the sleep from her eyes, smearing the dirt on her tear-streaked face.

"Mama? Mama!" She exclaimed with joy. "Oh, Mama!" She wrapped her arms tightly around Rahab and squeezed as hard as she could. "Mama, I was so scared." She began to sob. "I couldn't find you."

"I know, baby. I know. I was scared, too." Rahab stroked Lily's braids. "But don't worry, baby. I have you now, and I'll never let you go." Rahab picked her up and started for home. "I love you, Lily."

"I know, Mama. I love you, too."

Once they were home, Rahab's excitement returned when their household furnishings were delivered. She and Lily spent the rest of the day putting their home in order, arranging and rearranging it until the furniture and wall hangings were perfect.

Rahab enjoyed spending time with Lily. She needed to find a job, but she gave herself one week to spend time with Lily, savoring their precious time together

Stepping out onto the busy streets, she wondered where to begin her search. She decided to start at one end of the market, stopping at every vendor, until she was hired. Rahab started off on her search immediately. She pushed through the bustling streets, a specific purpose in her step. At every place, she heard the same story, they were not hiring. She knew dragging Lily along with her cut down on her chances, but she had no one to leave Lily with.

Hours later, worn out and feeling dejected, she trudged into one last business. "Are you looking to hire?" Rahab asked.

Without turning around, the proprietor answered, "Of course! Everyone is looking to hire these days."

"But everywhere I've been, they tell me they're not hiring."

The man turned to look at Rahab. "Oh. Sorry. I was mistaken. I'm not hiring after all."

"You just told me you are!" Rahab objected.

The man stared hard at her. "Not to the likes of you."

"The likes of me? What's that supposed to mean?"

"Every man in Jericho knows who you are," the proprietor explained. "Every man in Jericho has received services from the most notable prostitute in Astarte's temple."

Rahab gasped, placing her hand to her chest.

The man grinned. "What? You didn't know you were everyone's favorite?"

Rahab had no idea. No wonder she seemed to be so much busier than the rest of the girls. It *wasn't* just in her head as she'd thought. Rahab was disgusted. Everyone's favorite.

No one would hire her. What would she do? What *could* she do? Suddenly an idea began to form in her mind, just the hint of an idea. Just a spark. The faintest flicker of hope.

Chapter 8

Over the next few days, Rahab's idea continued to bounce around in her mind. There weren't very many inns on her end of town. Maybe she could pull it off. Her house was big enough; she had plenty of rooms. Her home was thoroughly furnished and decorated. All she needed was to let people know she was open for business.

What would she call her inn? Rahab's Inn. No. Made her sound haughty. Jericho's Hub. Sounded like a brothel. Center Street Inn. Too generic. Center Inn. Perfect! It captured the street name, let people know where it was, and was also catchy and rang with a second meaning. It spoke of setting your sights on something. Center Inn. Yes! Perfect!

She opened her doors immediately and started spreading the word. Gossip and news traveled quickly in Jericho. Just to make sure everyone knew of Center Inn, she stopped as many people traveling down the street as she could to tell them the news—there was now another inn available for weary travelers. Center Inn offered full meals, something no other inn offered, and also served as a restaurant for local people.

A few mornings later, her hopes high, Rahab threw open the door to her home to let in the fresh air. She breathed deeply and smiled, picking up a broom and started sweeping pesky cobwebs out of the corner nearest the door.

"So, it is true!" Rahab heard a familiar voice behind her, turned she saw two of her closest friends from the temple standing in the doorway.

"Gina! Ira!" She ran to greet them. They all three tangled in a warm embrace.

"Life sure seems to be treating you well." Gina looked Rahab looked over, her light brown eyes dancing. "And look at this place!"

"I heard you opened an inn, but I wasn't sure whether to believe it." Ira's curly locks bounced as she shook her head. "You, opening an inn. I would never have thought it."

"At least you've got work." Gina looked at the floor. "We can't find anything. Nothing."

"No one will have us." Ira sighed, her whole chunky frame wilting in defeat. "Because we were temple prostitutes."

"You've come to the right place. I have positions for both of you." First, Rahab smiled at Gina. "I need a maid, someone to clean up after the guests." Then she smiled at Ira. "And I need a cook."

At the temple, Ira had gloated about how good she could cook. Her food was the best in the city, she always said. Now was her chance to prove it.

Gina and Ira started talking at once. Of course, they would accept the positions. They needed something, and what better job than to work for a good friend?

"I can't pay you, though," Rahab admitted. "Not until I start getting business."

"Don't worry about it," said Ira, waving her hand. "My parents have been feeding us both and housing us, too."

"Being a temple prostitute did not bring my parents prosperity as Astarte promised." Gina kicked at a raised area in the floor where three rocks met. "They're still so poor they can't afford to support me. Thankfully, Ira's parents took me in. I don't know what I'd do without them."

Her friends hugged her again and set off to Ira's parent's house to pack their things and move into Center Inn. Rahab watched them leave, a spring in their steps now, and thought of Orb. Still stuck in the temple because she had nowhere else to go.

That afternoon, Rahab used some of her dwindling funds to purchase five tables and chairs. She chose round tables, a new innovation, which made her inn appear sleek and modern. She had chandeliers installed over the tables, expensive chandeliers with ten candles in each. They were held with long chains that reached to the walls and worked on a pulley system that allowed the chandeliers to be lowered and raised to make the candles accessible for lighting and changing.

Everything was ready, but no one came. No one. No one came for food. No one came for lodging. *Why,* Rahab wondered, *Everything is in order. My inn is the only one that offers food and the only restaurant with the newer tables.* She thought people would come, if for nothing else than to see the tables. *Surely my past isn't affecting this, too!*

Two weeks passed, and still, no one came. Rahab began to worry. Her funds were shrinking. Something had to change, and soon. At this rate, she and Lily would be starving paupers by the end of the month. Ira and Gina had brought some food with them, sent as a gift by Ira's parents, but soon that, too, would be gone. And she still had no money to pay their wages.

I could offer my body for hire, but I promised myself I'd never do that again.

Even so, Rahab realized there really was an opportunity here for a lucrative business, but she couldn't. She just couldn't. She could only watch as her funds grew slimmer and slimmer.

If only there was another way. Maybe someone will come soon.

Every day, Rahab watched the door. She still had her hopes, although they were waning. She sat at the table nearest the door, facing the door. Hoping. She grew thinner and thinner, trying to stretch their food, trying to make sure there was enough for Lily.

One morning Rahab noticed the shadows under Lily's once glowing eyes. Her little shoulders, once carried proud and high, began to droop. She didn't play or run through the house; she sat still and wan. *She has no energy*, Rahab realized, *she needs more food.*

There was only enough food left for one more week if Rahab didn't eat. That made her decision for her.

There was no other way to support herself and Lily, no other way to provide honest work to her friends Gina and Ira. Using her new house—her precious home—in such a way made her feel ill, but she was out of options. This time, she vowed, it would be on her own terms. Her home would be an inn for weary travelers, yes, but also a draw to local men.

An inn with an added bonus—a harlot at their beckon and call. Since she'd been "everyone's favorite" at the temple, she was sure her new business would be lucrative. Word shouldn't take as long to spread this time.

Defeated, Rahab purchased a long scarlet cord and wrapped it around the pole in front of her home, covering it from top to bottom to show what she was offering, a harlot for a price.

Rahab needed someone to watch Lily, someone to care for her while she entertained her male customers. Most of her business would take place at night, but she would need to sleep part of the day. She needed someone she could trust. But who?

"Gina, I have a question." Rahab approached her friend the next day. "I need someone to look after Lily while I entertain gentleman callers. Is it too much to ask you to look after her while I'm working or sleeping?"

"Not at all. I'd be happy to, Rahab," Gina replied with a smile. "I'm so grateful to you for helping Ira and me."

News of Rahab's new business venture buzzed around town. Women whispered with disdain and shunned her.

Men shook their heads in front of their wives and talked excitedly about it as soon as their backs were turned. Everyone knew the big brick house on top of the walls. Everyone knew where Rahab lived, where she could be found.

Rahab quickly got used to the whispering behind her back. She heard fragments here and there. Fragments of conversations she was supposed to hear, said for her benefit, and fragments she overheard by accident.

"Glad to hear the girl has come to her senses," said the owner of the market who had refused her a job less than a year before. "She's finally doing what comes best to her. Once a whore, always a whore."

Rahab bristled. She knew what he'd meant, but it wasn't true. She was a person with good points and bad points, just like anyone else. She was more than *just* a whore. And she would prove it. Somehow.

Two days later, her first customer walked in. His clothing, a long flowing silken robe held by a purple sash, suggested wealth. His sandals were new, clean, and tied around his ankles and lower leg in the newest fashion of the day. She should be able to fetch a handsome price from this one. Handsome indeed. She smiled a light, seductive smile. She rose from her seat near the window and walked toward him, a sway in her step.

"Well, hello there." Her words dripped like honey from her lips.

She hated the shake of her hips, the walk of a harlot. The walk she'd learned while she was a temple prostitute.

The man stepped out of the sunlight shrouding his face. The light had made it impossible to see his features. A wicked smile was plastered on the man's face. It was Yassib.

Rahab was taken aback. She had never thought of this possibility, this horror. Seeing the shocked look on her face, Yassib laughed a sadistic laugh.

"Hello yourself," he taunted. "Come on, whore. Show me some good time."

Rahab boiled inside but quickly regained her composure. She couldn't afford to turn him away. She had to serve him. She had to give him what he wanted just as she had done at the temple—but this time, it would be on her terms. She had promised herself that—it would be her terms. Rahab straightened her shoulders and looked Yassib in the eye.

"This is not the temple, Yassib. This is my home. You speak to me, respectfully, or you may take your business elsewhere."

"Respectfully!" Yassib gave a shout of mocking laughter. "You're a whore."

"I am a businesswoman," Rahab replied coolly, despite the anger burning inside her. "No one commands me here. Not even Astarte."

"That's blasphemy. And I like it." A leer crossed Yassib's face. "Come here, wh—I mean, Mistress Rahab."

"No. You come here." Rahab gave him a smile and turned away, sashaying toward the staircase that led to the bedrooms upstairs.

Maybe she could murder him and make it look like an accident, she thought furiously. Maybe—another day. Today, she needed his money.

"Coming?" Rahab placed her hand on the banister and looked back at Yassib. She pulled at her loose neckline, allowing her robe to slip over her shoulder, effectively showing just enough to tantalize any customer. "I'll be waiting for you."

Chapter 9

The day dawned bright and cheery. The fifth day of the fifth month. Rahab had always liked days that repeated the number of their month. They somehow felt like lucky days. Things always went well for her on repeating days. Today would be a good day. Perhaps a special day, like the day twelve months ago when she'd bought her home.

Business was booming. People came for lodging. People came for food. Men came for her services. She could turn away anyone she wanted and still want for nothing. She could even afford to turn Yassib away now, and she had a time or two. It drove him mad, but he always came back. When he did, he offered her twice the price. Then she would smile and accept.

Today was Saturday, her day off. She decided to take Lily on a walk to the marketplace. Rahab did not do the household shopping. That was part of Ira's duties. As the cook, she knew what she needed.

The marketplace was crowded as usual, but it somehow didn't seem as dusty, and the heat didn't seem as stifling. The conversations going on around her seemed clearer and more distinct than they usually did.

She didn't feel rushed. She felt peaceful. It was a perfect day.

"I can't believe Hagdad is finally getting married! I honestly didn't think anyone would ever betroth that girl!"

At the mention of her sister's name, Rahab came to an abrupt stop, turned her head and tuned her ears on the conversation between two women at a fruit vendor's stall. "I heard the news this afternoon," said the woman whose voice had caught Rahab's attention. "Right after lunch."

Excitement filled Rahab. Her sister was getting married! The custom was for children to marry in order from oldest to youngest, but since Rahab had been disowned by her family, Hagdad, being the next oldest, was free to marry. *Why is she marrying so late in life? She must be twenty by now. That's six years too late! Girls usually married around fourteen. Everyone was married by sixteen. Maybe she matured later in life? Maybe my leaving sent her into a dark depression that caused no one to want her? Or maybe my prostitution; maybe my reputation made her undesirable. It's all my fault! If only I hadn't signed on with the temple.*

Rahab's shoulders felt heavy with regret. She was the reason her sister had not found happiness. *Who wants to wed the sister of a harlot?* Poor Hagdad.

Rahab tried to imagine how Hagdad must feel. She wouldn't know her betrothed. Not really. She wouldn't have chosen her husband. That was done for her. Rahab was the only person Hagdad talked to growing up, but Rahab had stolen that from her, too. She hoped her sister had found someone else to confide in.

Rahab longed to be there for Hagdad at her wedding. To be there with her. If only—No. She wouldn't let "if-onlies" stand in her way and run her life.

Rahab would never be welcomed at the small family gathering, but she had to try! For Hagdad.

Rahab looked up. A full moon hung high in the sky opposite the bright sun. Astarte's blessing on her sister's wedding. *Perhaps Astarte will smile kindly on me too, and my family will allow me to join in the wedding celebration,* Rahab thought sarcastically. She knew Astarte didn't hear her prayers. Still, she could hope.

By eavesdropping on the marketplace gossip, Rahab learned the ceremony was today, that it was to be held in a well-known place between the inner and outer walls. Hurrying, Lily beside her, she walked there, waiting with trepidation for her family to arrive.

Hagdad had chosen the perfect place, she thought. It was a clearing right outside the city. The trees that surrounded it were full of pink blossoms, and there was a Tamarisk tree near the center that was overflowing with the beautiful pink blossoms too. She wondered if the ceremony would be held under that tree where fallen petals decorated the lush, dark grass, a soft carpet.

Hagdad was the first person she saw, walking slowly, by herself, toward the lovely Tamarisk tree. Rahab saw uncertainty and anxiety in her eyes.

Rahab walked slowly toward her. "Hagdad," she said quietly.

Hagdad jerked her head up at the sound of her sister's voice. Rahab saw surprise, then confusion, and then joy travel across Hagdad's face.

"Rahab!" She squealed and ran toward Rahab, arms open wide. "Oh, Rahab! I never imagined you'd be here. I wanted you here so badly, so did Levi, but I knew you couldn't come."

"Who's Levi?" Rahab asked.

"My betrothed." Hagdad blushed prettily. "The pot merchant's son. You remember him."

"Of course." Rahab smiled, even though she did not. "I'm so happy for you."

"Rahab! What in Astarte's name are you doing here?" Rahab felt a hand roughly grasp her shoulder a moment before her father spun her around to face him, his face flushed. "You are not welcome here! You are never allowed around my family!"

He grabbed Hagdad's arm and yanked her behind him. "Leave now."

Rahab had hoped, especially with the warm reception from Hagdad, that her family had forgiven her. She'd hoped she had a chance. But all her hopes were gone. Dashed. Shattered.

"I see you have a bastard child," Rahab's father sneered. "The child of a harlot doomed to become a harlot herself."

Rahab's temper flared. How dare he talk to her that way! About Lily!

She felt her hand come up. She felt the air move as she whipped her hand toward him. She felt the impact. Heard the slap. Still, she couldn't believe she had slapped her father in the face. Now all her hopes were truly gone. Forever.

The shock that registered on his face mirrored Rahab's. Then his expression quickly returned to hatred and disgust.

"Lily is an innocent child," Rahab said with all the calm she could muster. "Leave *your granddaughter* out of this."

Before her father could insult her or Lily again, Rahab took her daughter's hand and led her away. What now? She'd really wanted to see Hagdad's wedding. She could watch from a distance. They couldn't stop her from doing that! When she'd walked what she considered to be far enough up the hill to be undisturbed, Rahab sat down in the shade under a large sycamore tree and drew Lily into her lap.

She wondered what was being said about her and Lily. Were they still calling Lily a bastard? Were they talking about Rahab slapping her father? She really had reacted badly. Striking her father. What was she thinking?

Rahab saw Levi walking toward Hagdad. His tall stature made his stride long. He was thin and well kept. His black hair was cut close to his head. His skin was lighter than Hagdad's, but not by much. His smile was large and bright. He looked excited about this marriage, his prize.

The wedding started like every other wedding in Jericho, with prayers of praise and asking a blessing from Astarte. Rahab smirked at the prayers. Astarte didn't care. *We could definitely have a better god! If she cared, my life would have been better. She wouldn't have allowed me to rip myself from my family. She wouldn't have allowed me to hurt my family. To hurt Hagdad.*

As Hagdad and her espoused took their place in the center of the circle of candles, the priest took his place in front of the couple. Rahab knew what was said and done at weddings. She'd been to a few before joining the temple, two of her cousins and one aunt.

She imagined what the priest might be saying. "We are here today to join Levi and Hagdad in a holy pact before Astarte."

She watched as Hagdad and Levi moved closer together and joined hands. Levi leaned toward her, saying something. Hagdad lowered her head with an embarrassed smile. What had he said? Rahab wished she were closer.

Hagdad and Levi began speaking to each other aloud. Rahab could barely hear their voices, let alone make out what was being said. She knew they were exchanging vows. She imagined what they might say. "I promise to hold and cherish Hagdad in a way that honors Astarte. I promise to keep myself only to her and to keep myself pure in the honor and service of Astarte."

Hagdad would reply, "I promise to honor Levi. I promise to obey him in everything he wills in the honor and service of Astarte."

On the gentle breeze, Rahab heard Levi and Hagdad murmur, "Amen and amen."

They embraced, join hands, and floated off together to consummate their marriage. At their home, they'd make their marriage official with each other and in the eyes of Astarte.

Rahab wondered how long it would be before Hagdad would be holding a baby of her own. It usually didn't take long after a wedding before the wife became pregnant. Hagdad deserved happiness.

Rahab couldn't undo what she'd done. The past was gone, the present was something she'd have to endure, but the future was hers for the taking. She was the master of her own life. She'd stolen Hagdad's sister, her friend, and her confidant from her. She'd lost her place in Hagdad's life. That grieved Rahab, but she wouldn't mourn the past.

Rahab's present? Her father wouldn't let her forget that she'd left, but she'd made a name for herself despite his abuse. She was a woman of means. She owned property and ran a successful business. She could afford to give Hagdad whatever she wanted. And so, Rahab vowed, she would do so, whether she had her father's blessing or not.

Chapter 10

"They're coming here next!" A chunky woman seated on one side of the dining room exclaimed, nodding her head so vigorously her dark brown topknot of hair bobbed up and down.

"Oh, don't be so dramatic," her tall lunch companion answered, her hair up in braids and her skin the color of almonds. "You can't know that."

"I do know it; I had a dream," the chunky woman replied. "And you know it too. You usually practically devour your food, but you've not touched it. You're not yourself today, Dorty. *Something* is weighing on your mind."

"You know me too well, Tara." The almond-skinned woman looked down at her weathered hands. "I admit I'm a little nervous. I hear a lot of people talking, and they seem so sure."

"What are we talking about, ladies?" Rahab asked as she poured more water into their half-empty glasses.

Today she was helping the new girl, Merkah, serve luncheon. It was Merkah's first day, so she was understandably slow, but the rush of people didn't slow down for anyone.

"You haven't heard?" the woman named Tara asked. "Israel is coming this way! Some say Jericho is their next target! After what they did to Egypt and leaving so many conquered cities in their wake, people are worried and frightened."

Rahab knew about Israel. Who didn't? They'd conquered Egypt without lifting a hand and left the entire country devastated and destitute. She'd heard that the people of Israel mocked the Egyptian gods through every plague that descended on the pharaoh and his people. Some said Israel's God did it for them.

Rahab didn't believe any god would fight for his people. Astarte, supposedly the goddess of war, certainly didn't. Rahab wasn't sure she even believed there was a god anymore, but if there was and she could have her pick, she'd choose a god like Israel's God, a God that supposedly loved and fought for His people.

From Egypt, Israel had gone on to conquer many other lands, some because they didn't help Israel and some because their God told them to. It was said that their God had led them out of Egypt in the form of a pillar of cloud during the day and a pillar of fire at night.

Jericho was a major trade center of the region, so many people from many lands traveled through the city and spread their gossip. Rahab didn't believe most of it. Many stories were stretched beyond belief. This one probably was, too.

"Be at ease, ladies." Rahab set down her pitcher. "We live in Jericho, behind two strong and stout walls. And we have Astarte to protect us." She snickered under her breath. *Astarte. Whatever.*

"Of course, of course." Tara's companion, Dorty, sighed. "Thank you, Rahab."

Bowing her head, Rahab left the table. In the year since it opened, the fame of Center Inn and its wonderful cook had spread throughout the city. Rarely was Rahab shunned these days; in the marketplace now and then, but here in her own inn she was treated with respect. Tara and Dorty, two ladies of means, were some of her best customers.

Rahab returned to the kitchen to fill her pitcher, still thinking of Israel.

She'd heard other stories claiming that the people of Israel carried their god with them in a big golden box. The ark of God, they called it, was a personification of their God, a place where He showed up to lead them, a place where they worshipped Him with blood and burnt offerings. More burnt offerings. How many babies did *they* sacrifice? *No, thank you.*

As the weeks passed, the stories grew more outlandish and spread fear throughout Jericho. According to travelers who entered the city, Israel was definitely coming. Some inhabitants chose to leave Jericho; though most stayed, believing the city's thick walls and barred doors would keep any would-be attacker out. They were safe within their fortress.

Rahab secretly wished there *was* a way for Jericho to be destroyed, then the pigs she served at Center Inn would get their due. Yassib would get what he deserved. But there was no way anyone could ever penetrate the fortress of Jericho. It would never happen.

One night, as she sat in the front room enjoying the beauty of the sunset—reds, violets, and oranges—Rahab saw something moving in the shadows—or someone. As she watched closely, she realized it was two men prowling around outside. What could they be after? *If they've come to cause trouble, they're in the wrong place.*

Rahab rose and moved toward the door. On her way, she reached for a long, thick stick someone had left standing in the corner, and moved out into the street. *Now, where did they go?*

Stick held high, she moved into the alley at the side of the house. *Aha! There you are.*

"Can I help you?" She demanded in the deepest, boldest voice she could muster.

The two men, hunched as they melted from shadow to shadow, jumped and started to back away.

"Who are you?" Rahab demanded.

"Just two weary travelers," one answered in a low gravelly voice.

"Then you must be looking for lodging," Rahab began to feel bolder, but kept her stick held high in a way she hoped was threatening.

No one looked for lodging in an alley. They were up to no good. She looked around warily, searching for a third man that might be lurking in the shadows.

"We were planning to leave this evening," the man continued, "but we were trapped inside the city walls when the gates closed for the night."

Anyone could leave the city if they just went through the guards. Seasoned travelers knew that. Something was wrong here. *Lawbreakers? Escapees from the city prison? Someone just up to no good? Or...* She knew Israel was coming. Could these be spies? Spies from Israel?

Excitement built inside Rahab. If they truly were spies, she would do everything she could to help them. But how could she know for sure? In the dwindling light, she could see that they had olive-colored skin. She'd not seen anyone with skin of that color in a long time.

"It's getting dark fast. Aren't you scared to be out at this time of night?" Rahab asked. "There are evil characters moving about."

The two men looked at each other. "God will take care of us."

I knew it! Rahab exalted. Spies from Israel.

"Come with me." She lowered her voice and motioned with her hand for them to follow.

Andrew glanced at Salmon, a questioning look mixed with trepidation. Salmon wondered what Andrew was thinking and if Andrew felt as leery as he did. *God told Joshua to send us,* Salmon thought. *He wouldn't bring us here and then slay us.*

Andrew followed the woman, so Salmon followed her too. There was nothing else he could do. He had to trust God.

She quietly led them to the opposite side of the house and up the stairs to the rooftop. Her dark skin made it difficult to follow her as she slipped through the darkness.

"I'm sorry I don't have any rooms available," she said in a whisper, something like regret edging her voice.

"This will do," Andrew replied, keeping his voice low.

Salmon couldn't believe it. God was proving Himself again. He was providing them with a safe place for the night.

He and Andrew had come to Jericho to scout out the land for Joshua. Taking Jericho seemed impossible to Salmon. The inner wall was so thick that entire houses, like this one, were built on top of it with room left for a road. Both walls seemed impregnable with no weak spots.

Now this woman was helping them. Could she be an angel sent by God?

Stepping toward the center of the roof to conceal the light, Rahab lit the lamp she kept on a bench near the roof's edge. Now, she could see the men's features. One was large, well built, and tall. His disheveled hair made him look comical in the shadows cast by the lamp. The other man was of average size and scrawny. He couldn't be over twenty-five but carried himself with the air of a much older and more confident man.

"You can sleep under the booth." She pointed to a small building near the center of the roof with four open sides and roofed with dried palm leaves. "I don't think it'll rain tonight."

"Thank you," said the well-built man in a husky voice, "but we can't pay you."

"Be sure to destroy Jericho completely," Rahab whispered with a smile, "and that will be payment enough."

She heard the men gasp.

"How did you know?" the lanky man asked.

"It wasn't hard to figure out, but don't worry. I won't turn you in," Rahab whispered.

"It's probably best if you put out the light but be careful if you move around up here in the dark. There's a pile of flax by the fire pit you could trip over, and there are benches around the fire pit. Those would make a lot of racket. Rest well."

She nodded to the two men and quietly walked away. It was time to slip into a few rooms and play the harlot. If Israel defeated Jericho, perhaps she would not have to for much longer.

After her duties, Rahab retired to her room. She tried to sleep, but couldn't get her mind off the two spies. She tossed and turned and finally went outside for some fresh air hoping it would make her drowsy. She would normally go up onto the top of her roof, but she didn't want to wake the spies. Instead, she walked around the outside of the house and up and down the road on the top of the wall.

On the verge of dawn, she finally felt tired enough to sleep. She turned toward the house, then stopped abruptly when she heard a loud banging at the front door.

"Open up, Rahab!" The voice was definitely masculine. Who could that be?

Rahab rushed toward her house. He would awaken her customers if she didn't hurry.

"Yes?" It was Ira's voice. Sweet Ira, answering the door.

"The City Watch," the man replied. From the metallic cling against the rock wall, Rahab guessed he wasn't alone. "I know they're here."

"Who?" Ira asked, bewildered. "Who's here?"

"Where's Rahab?" the soldier demanded. "She may not know it, but there are Israelite spies hiding in her inn."

Rahab gasped, stopped, and knelt in a dark shadow out of sight from the soldiers. What would she do? If they found the spies, they'd kill them! If they found she was purposely hiding the spies, they'd kill her!

Salmon heard rushed footsteps tripping up the stairs to the roof. Light footsteps. A woman. Not the loud men he'd heard near the front of the house.

"Hurry!" The woman of the house whispered frantically. "The soldiers are at the door! We have to hide you!"

Salmon heard the men, the soldiers, shouting inside the inn, ordering people out of their rooms so they could be searched. They would search the entire house, including the roof.

"That's it!" The woman whispered excitedly, staring at the flax stalks. "Come on! Get into the fire pit! Get in," she repeated in a commanding tone.

Her black skin, shimmering in the light, somehow added to her air of authority. Salmon and Andrew climbed in. There was room enough for both to huddle below the rim. Just barely. The woman quickly spread the flax stalks over them to cover the hole. If she spread it out well enough, she might be able to convince the soldiers she'd laid the flax out to dry.

He heard heavy footsteps climbing the rooftop steps. *She better hurry!*

"Rahab. There you are," said one of the soldiers.

Rahab recognized him as one of her regular nighttime visitors and turned to face him with a smile.

"Hello, Melhum. To what do I owe the pleasure?"

"What are you doing up here?" Melhum demanded.

"I came up here for some fresh air. Is it a crime to walk on one's own rooftop?"

"A neighbor saw you taking two suspicious men into the inn last night. There are some spies loose in the city. We're certain the men you took in last night were the spies."

"Oh, my!" Rahab raised her hand to her mouth in mock shock, hopeful that it would convince the soldiers. "I would have never guessed! They were so polite and paid so well that I didn't ask any questions."

"So, they *are* here?"

"They *were* here. They're not any longer. They left just after I woke up and spoke of leaving the city. If you hurry, you might be able to catch them!"

Rahab waited with bated breath, hoping they would believe her. She searched their faces. In the shadows of the rising sun, she read both surprise and haste. They'd be in a hurry to report their findings to their captain. They rushed down the steps back to their post.

She couldn't risk staying on the roof any longer. Someone might report her activities as suspicious. Perhaps the same person who had reported to the authorities in the first place.

"You heard what he said. I must go," Rahab said to the spies, barely moving her lips, and not daring to look at the fire pit in case someone was watching from a nearby rooftop. "I'm sorry to leave you there, but I think you'll be safe. I'll be back at nightfall."

Chapter 11

For what little remained of the night, until the sun slowly peeked over the horizon, Rahab lay awake in her bed, listening. Every noise she heard in the street made her jump. Every snore from one of her guests, every footfall as another got up to use the chamber pot had her springing to her feet, her heart pounding.

When she heard the girls she'd hired to fetch water for Ira come, singing, back from the well with their jars of water, Rahab rose from her bed, exhausted and worried. She washed and changed her robe, pulled her braids back into a tail at the nape of her neck, and strapped on her sandals.

What if the soldiers come back? she wondered on her way down the stairs. What will happen to Lily? Maybe I should turn the spies in. Pretend I accidentally found them hiding on my roof. I would be safe. And even rewarded.

All the while, Rahab knew she couldn't do that. The Israelites were the answer to her prayers, and her integrity wouldn't allow it. *But I have to plan for Lily. She has to be cared for.*

She sent the oldest of the water girls with a message to Hagdad. They'd been secretly meeting in the marketplace during corresponding shopping trips. After

Rahab bought Hagdad and Levi a small plot of good farming ground, complete with a house, he'd been more than willing to allow Hagdad and Rahab to meet. Their father still refused to see Rahab.

Every bump in the house, every time the door opened, every shuffle of feet made Rahab jump, certain it was a soldier coming to take her away. *Please let me get everything set up for Lily first,* she prayed silently, hoping someone out there would hear.

At the midday meal, she sneaked out of the house and headed for the marketplace, veil in place just in case any of Hagdad's friends happened to see them together. She always kept her face covered when they met. Just in case.

When Rahab arrived at the market, Hagdad was waiting, pacing outside the weaver's shop where they always met. When she saw Rahab, she rushed to embrace her as she would a friend she met on the street.

"What is it, Rahab?" Hagdad asked, a questioning look on her face. Rightly so. Rahab had never sent for her before.

"We need to find a place to talk," said Rahab. "Someplace where no one will hear us."

"The alley," Hagdad suggested, and Rahab followed her to a dark corner far from the bustle of the street.

Wooden crates were stacked, four and five crates tall on either side of the alley. A small dark animal ran for cover behind one of the crates as they approached. *Rats.* The air smelled musty and stale. The breeze from the street did not reach here, which made the heat even more stifling.

Hagdad looked at Rahab. Waiting. Rahab knew Hagdad would never tell her secret. Not even to Levi, but she feared putting her sister in danger. She must protect Hagdad as well as Lily.

"If anything happens to me," Rahab said in a low voice, "promise me you'll take care of my Lily."

"Nothing is going happen to you," Hagdad replied in a comforting tone. Hagdad took Rahab's hand in hers and stroked it with her other hand.

"You don't know that. No one can know that." Rahab paused and looked around. She felt like someone was watching her. "I have to go. Just promise me."

"All right, but nothing is going to happen to you." Hagdad was more emphatic than comforting this time. "Are you in trouble?"

Hagdad's expression showed concern. And something more. Suspicion? What if Hagdad went to the authorities, thinking it would help her?

"I'll simply feel better if I know Lily will always be taken care of, just in case."

Hagdad's eyes narrowed. "Is Yassib threatening you again?"

Perfect, Rahab thought, lifting a maybe yes, maybe no shoulder. *Let her think it's Yassib.* She drew a leather moneybag from inside her cloak and pressed it into Hagdad's hands. "This is for Lily's care," she said.

"Rahab, I can't—"

"Take it, Hagdad!" Rahab's tone dared her sister to argue. "Hold it for Lily. In case. I have to go."

Rahab turned away, but Hagdad held fast to her hand and pulled her back around. Rahab saw worry on Hagdad's face. She started to say something, then sighed. "I promise."

"Thank you." Rahab gave her sister a quick hug. "Thank you."

That evening, an hour past full dark, Rahab walked up to the rooftop. Perspiration gathered upon her brow. She carried a small platter heaped with yeasty bread, grapes, and cheese. She hadn't dared to ask Ira for two plates.

She settled on one of the benches, nibbling a piece of cheese as she gazed idly around to make sure no one was watching. Then she carried the plate to the fire pit, set it aside and knelt to lift the flax stalks. She glanced around again, toward the east to make sure no one was watching and saw a towering glow, like that of fire. There was no way a fire could get that big or glow that brightly. What was it?

Rahab remembered the stories of the God of Israel. *The pillar of fire.* She had seen dark clouds to the east for three days, yet there was no rain. The fired glowed where the clouds had been during the day. Despite the warm night, Rahab felt a chill. Was she looking at the God of Israel?

Salmon stirred slightly, his joints screaming to be stretched. He and Andrew had been wedged into the fire pit since early that morning. Suddenly, he heard cautious footsteps coming toward them. Then he heard the flax rustling. He blinked and saw the light of the stars in the night sky above. *At last.* He breathed a sigh of relief and winced as he crawled out of the well. Everything hurt.

The dark-skinned woman placed a large oval plate of grapes, cheese, and bread between them. Salmon and Andrew thanked her and devoured the food.

"I'm sorry," the woman said, a sad edge to her voice. "I should've brought more."

"This will suffice, mistress. We thank you." Andrew wiped his hands on his robe. "My name is Andrew, and this," he motioned toward Salmon with an upturned palm, "is Salmon."

"Rahab."

Rahab, Salmon thought. *Such a beautiful name.*

"How did you get here? Over the Jordan, I mean?" The woman, Rahab, picked up the plate. "The waters overflow the banks this time of year, and the current is very swift."

"The water was only to our chest," Salmon said, "and the surface was still as glass."

Her eyes widened. "That's not possible!"

"It's true," said Andrew.

"I almost lost Emma, one of my sisters, to that current." Rahab brushed the crumbs off the plate into the fire pit. "I took the children to the Jordan for a picnic. Mother said not to get close, so I reminded them to stay far from the water. Emma didn't listen. Emma never listened. She wandered toward the bank and dropped her little yellow rag doll in the water. Her favorite doll. It was instantly swept away in the current. She jumped in to save it. Thankfully I saw her and was able to grab her robe."

"God blessed us," Salmon said, "with a quick-witted woman."

Rahab smiled a little but lifted one eyebrow. "I can see the Jordan from my roof. Just barely, but I can. Even from here, I can see the white water."

"I'm telling you. It was chest-high and slow moving," Andrew repeated. "Our God has a wonderful way of working miracles for us."

Miracles? Rahab thought about all the stories she had heard about Israel. It was a miracle that Andrew and Salmon hadn't been found. Melhum was a very thorough man. He had turned every room in her inn upside down searching for the spies, yet he didn't touch the flax.

"Everyone in Jericho is scared of you. Of Israel," Rahab said. "Everyone fears you'll defeat Jericho. I think you might. The God that defeated Egypt might be able to also defeat Jericho."

"How can we get out of the city?" Salmon asked. "We can't exactly walk out the gates."

"Let me think," Rahab replied.

The secret tunnels under the temple of Astarte led beyond the outside of the wall, but there was no way she could get them into the tunnels without being seen by someone. Unless…

"I know of some tunnels that run under the entire city and past the outer wall. I don't know all the passages, but my friend Orb does. She can help us. Come with me."

Rahab led the spies to the temple, stealing quietly from shadow to shadow, taking every alley she knew. The temple of Astarte and its beautiful gardens lay still and peaceful in the dark.

"Stay here." Rahab rushed off toward Orb's dorm, hoping she still lived in the same place.

She slipped soundlessly into the building and along the corridor to Orb's chamber. The temple was as she remembered it, simply and prettily furnished. A lamp burned low, and Orb sat cross-legged on her pallet, humming as she mended a hem.

"Orb," Rahab called softly to her from the doorway.

Her look of surprise quickly brightened into a big smile. She sprang off her pallet, and they embraced long and endearingly.

"Anything for my Rahab," Orb said quietly.

Taking Orb's hand, Rahab led her out into the gardens where she'd left the spies in hiding. The dew-dampened grass whisked beneath their sandals.

"Orb, I need your help and your knowledge of the tunnels to help these men out of the city. For your safety, please don't ask any questions."

Orb nodded her head. She stood staring at the spies for just a moment, then turned quickly and walked toward the temple. They crept along the wall, keeping close for added cover. Turning a corner, they abruptly came upon a tall and lush potted plant, full of bright red flowers. Beside it stood a side door into the temple.

Inside the temple, it was darker yet. Rahab and the spies silently followed Orb, who was barely visible in the dark. They wove around corners and in and out of doors for what seemed like forever. Finally, they came upon a trap door in the floor, which Orb pulled open as quietly as she could. The small squeak of the hinges could not be helped.

Looking around, Orb reached out and drew Rahab into a tight embrace. She held her out from her by the shoulders, then pulled her in for another short hug.

"It's a straight shot from here," Orb whispered. "Take a right at every fork except the third one. There you make a left. The only deviation is that you'll make a left at the third fork." Orb looked into Rahab's eyes, tears filling her own. "Good luck."

"Wait! You're not coming with us?"

"I can't. I promised to meet my friend Angel tonight. I'm already late." Orb stepped back. "If I don't show up soon, she's the kind of person who will come looking."

Rahab nodded her head, then she and the spies turned to go, eager to get on their way.

The tunnels were dark and cold. Moisture hung in the stale air. They could hear every little noise. Even the sound of their footfalls bounced off the walls. They began tiptoeing, being careful not to shuffle their feet. They breathed lightly. They walked softly around each turn, listening quietly for any movement. They were almost home free!

"Come on, Stauban!" Rahab heard a male voice jesting around the corner. "It'll be fun!"

She stopped short, the spies behind her. Salmon bumped her shoulder and pushed her forward half a step. Rahab tripped on a jutting stone and gave a sharp gasp before she could raise her hand to her mouth.

"What was that?" A worried voice came from around the corner.

Footsteps hurried toward Rahab and the spies. They flattened themselves against the cold rock walls. The footsteps and the flicker of a lamp drew closer. Rahab's heart began to pound.

"Don't worry about it, Stauban!" the first man called, a chuckle in his voice. "It's just your imagination. Your guilty conscience."

"I guess so," the second man sighed hesitantly.

The light stopped, wavered, and then retreated. Rahab and the two spies let out a breath they didn't know they were holding. At the sound of dice being shaken and thrown on the stone floor of the tunnel, Rahab sighed.

She turned in the darkness, gesturing for Salmon and Andrew to follow her back the way they'd come. They exited the tunnels, hurried through the temple gardens, and kept mostly to the alleys on their way to Rahab's house and back up the steps to the roof.

The only way out, Rahab decided, was over the wall. She walked to the edge her roof and peered down the side of her house. There were trees growing along the outside of the wall. Tall, sturdy trees. If they could only get over the walls to the trees, they'd be able to get down. How could they do that? It was too high a drop from the rooftop, but maybe if they went through a lower window of her house?

She thought another moment, then whispered. "Wait here."

She hurried down the steps and around to the front of her house. Quickly, she unwound the long red cord from the tall pole. She had forgotten what color the pole was. Now it gleamed bright brass still shiny from being covered so long.

She gathered the mass of rope in her arms and hurried to the rooftop to show it to Andrew and Salmon.

"A harlot," Salmon said, his voice sounding as though his heart had dropped into his sandals. His face showed disgust and then quickly changed to stone. "I'm sorry. I shouldn't have said that—"

Rahab tried to ignore his comment. It was the same thing she heard every day, but for some reason, it hurt more coming from him.

"I can use this to lower you down. It won't reach the ground, but it should be long enough for you to reach the tops of the trees that grow beside the wall." Rahab took a breath. "When you take Jericho, can you save my family? Can you keep them alive?"

"All I can promise," Andrew said hesitantly, "is that I'll ask."

"Yes," said Salmon firmly. "We can promise you that your family will be saved."

"You can't promise that, Salmon!" Andrew was aghast. "You can't speak for God. Or for Joshua, for that matter! How can you promise such a thing?"

"Because I know my God, Andrew. He mercifully spared whole cities simply because they helped us on our way. I have faith that He will do the same for Rahab. And I know Joshua. He is my great uncle, after all. He would want her spared, too."

"Very well," Andrew sighed, looking at Rahab. "But only under these conditions. One, you must not tell anyone we were here."

"No danger of that," said Rahab. "They'd have my head."

"Two," Andrew continued, "you must hang this cord in your window. The soldiers will be told to spare the lives of everyone in your house. Any of your family who is not in your house will be killed along with everyone else."

"Agreed," Rahab said, wondering how she would convince her family, especially her father, to enter her house. "This way."

She quietly led them inside and through the corridors to a large room at the back of the house. If they were quick, she could get them out the window before any of her customers knew anyone had come inside the house.

"Are you sure you'll be able to hold the rope for us to shimmy down?" Salmon asked.

"You can help me hold it while Andrew climbs down," Rahab suggested. "I'm sure I can hold it while you climb down."

Salmon looked apprehensive but picked up the end of the rope anyway. Andrew climbed over the wall and lowered himself into the tree below. When the rope went limp, Rahab knew it was Salmon's turn.

I can do this. I can do this, she chanted to herself. But truthfully, she didn't know for sure if she could or not.

Chapter 12

"Before you go," Rahab said.

Salmon turned toward her, shifting from foot to foot. He was impatient to be gone, and rightly so. If anyone saw him climbing down the wall, he and Andrew would be killed. He didn't want to waste time, but this woman had hidden them and saved their lives.

"Yes, mistress," he said. "What is it?"

"The soldiers are looking for you," Rahab told him. "Don't go directly back to the Israelite camp. Conceal yourselves in the hills. Wait there a few days, then continue to your camp. By then, the soldiers will have given up looking for you and returned to Jericho."

"Thank you," said Salmon. "We'll follow your advice."

Rahab tightly grasped her end of the rope and set herself to hold it for Salmon to climb down. She wrapped the rope loosely around her left arm and hand and held it directly in front of her left hand with her right. She spaced her feet evenly, her right foot in front of the other and further to the side. She braced her foot against the wall below the window.

She was breathing fast, her chest rising and falling quickly. She was biting her bottom lip, and her face was taut. Salmon looked her over, then set his mouth in a grim line. What had he gotten himself into? How safe would he really be dangling from the end of a rope with this slim woman holding the other end?

Suddenly, there was a shuffle behind them. They'd been found out! Rahab whirled toward the sound. A large figure was outlined in the doorway. She took a step backward toward the wall as a large figure moved toward her and Salmon. She felt a scream welling up in her throat. Panic gripped her, threatening to strangle her. A hand reached out and grabbed her by the shoulder. Then realization hit her.

"Orbid!" She sighed with relief. "You scared the fool out of me."

"Who is this person?" Salmon asked Rahab nervously.

"This is Orbid, my manservant. He's no threat. He is mute, but even if he could speak, he is very loyal to me. He wouldn't snitch even if he could." She smiled up at Orbid. "You came just in time."

Rahab handed Orbid her end of the rope. "Can you please hold this while Salmon," she motioned toward the Israelite spy, "climbs down the wall?"

Orbid nodded his head and quietly picked up the rope. His six-foot-two, muscular frame dwarfed Salmon, who stood beside him, staring at him in wonder. Orbid jerked his chin toward the window, motioning for Salmon to get going.

Belly down, Salmon scooted his legs over the ledge. Grasping the rope, he lowered himself slowly out the window. Rahab saw the rope go taut. Orbid's upper arm muscles rippled under his dark skin. Rahab peeked out the window and watched breathlessly as Salmon, hand over hand, his feet against the wall for support, shimmied down the rope as quickly as he could. When his feet were safely grounded on the nearest tree branch, Rahab finally let out her breath. With a wave to Rahab, he and Andrew started on their way.

Rahab watched with trepidation as they disappeared from sight under cover of darkness. Their skin, olive-colored, wasn't dark like Rahab's and wouldn't give them extra cover in the darkness.

"God, keep them safe," she prayed, hoping He was really there and that He would listen to her, a harlot.

How will I ever get my family to join me? To be safe?

Rahab fretted throughout the night, her second without much sleep. Late the next morning, she set out for her father's house, hoping that he would not be at home. If she could speak to her mother alone and convince her, perhaps she could convince her husband.

The sun didn't seem to shine as brightly today. The colors in people's clothing and in the tapestries hanging on the sides of buildings, usually sharp and vibrant, seemed dull and lifeless. The air felt heavy. The cloudless sky seemed to carry a message of doom. The lowing of the oxen, the bleating of the sheep, and the braying of the donkeys seemed far away. The palms and the flowing spring water used to irrigate the city didn't bring her the feeling of peace that they normally did. Her world felt like it was closing in on her. Would her mother listen to her?

She followed the city wall to the gate. It was crowded with travelers coming and going as always. Jericho was the center of commerce, so there was always a steady influx of people from many different regions. Some were coming to buy and sell, and some were coming to worship Astarte. Jericho's temple and devotion attracted many worshippers.

She headed through the gate, past the guards, standing tall and stately at attention, keenly aware of what was going on around them, and into the outer city of Jericho between the two walls.

Now that her family was living in outer Jericho, Rahab had worried about their safety, but housing was cheaper here since it didn't have as much protection as inner Jericho. As she walked, she thought about her old haunts—the flower fields and the river. A smile crossed her face as she remembered her special places. Inner Jericho had nothing on outer.

She knew she was getting close to her family's home when she smelled Crazy Mafta's goat farm. People called her that because she kept completely to herself. When people did chance to see her, she quickly hid from view. *Crazy.*

Rahab's family lived in the second house past the goat farm. A small house, but big enough. She knew where it was. She'd walked past it many times as a child on her way to gather flowers and herbs. Since she'd left the temple, she'd visited it from afar, careful not to be seen, so she could watch her younger siblings play. She missed them so.

Years ago, Rahab would have cut through the neighboring farms to get there quicker, but today she took the well-used road. Although she had dire news to share with her family, she was in no hurry. Anxiety tightened its grip on her as she drew closer. She hoped her mother and the rest of her family would listen but feared that they wouldn't.

A cluster of three stately palm trees that sat on the edge of the property loomed in front of her. She truly did miss her family. She'd missed them every day while she was in the temple. Old feelings washed over her as she came nearer. Nostalgia. Oh, to be with her family again.

The house was built of clay brick with a roof of thatched palm leaves. The front door barely hung on the house. *Father still hasn't fixed that.* She could see the curtain blowing lazily through the windows. Smells of the midday meal drifted to her. *Fry bread and beef.* Her stomach growled.

"Mother!" she called out. "Mother, are you home?"

The front door swung open, and her mother appeared in the doorway. *Mother.* She stood there without moving for a few seconds, and then she rushed toward Rahab, arms open wide. She nuzzled her face into Rahab's neck and began to weep. Rahab squeezed her back.

"It's so good to be home, Mother," she said, hugging her tightly.

Finally, her mother pushed herself away from Rahab, still holding her loosely around the neck. Tears still coursed down her flushed cheeks. "Oh! How I have missed you! Do come in."

Words Rahab had longed to hear. Still, she hesitated.

"Don't worry." Her mother smiled. "Your father's not here."

With a sigh of relief, Rahab followed her mother into the house. Her mother busied herself with the fry bread, flipping it over and checking the bottoms of the beef. Then she sat down on the heavy wooden seat and patted the empty place beside her.

"Emma got married," she told Rahab. "She's living in the old Aberstain's house in the middle of town. Married a soldier."

"Mother, I'm sorry I don't have time for small talk. I must be quick. Father will be home soon to eat.

Two Israelite spies showed up on my doorstep. They told me Israel is coming to conquer Jericho. They told me everyone who is inside my house when Israel comes will be safe."

"Oh, Rahab." Her mother gripped her hands. "Israel?"

"I helped them." Rahab held her mother's hands tightly in her lap. "They offered to protect my family in return. When Israel attacks, you must come to my house. You will be safe only with me, in my house. Do you understand? Come to my house, and you will be spared."

Rahab's mother nodded her head. Just barely.

"What is this?" Rahab's father bellowed from the doorway. "I told you to leave my family alone!" He moved toward her in big, threatening steps. Rahab stood just in time for her father to grab her arm, his grip like an iron vice, and yank her toward the door.

"It's true, Mother! You must believe me!" Rahab cried as her father pushed her out of the house. "Please, come!"

Her cries were cut short by the dilapidated door being slammed in her face. The door clung to its flimsy frame for only a second, then it broke loose and crashed to the ground, punctuating her father's tirade.

"Jericho lays within two walls. An outer wall about twenty-five feet high and an inner wall about forty-five feet high," Andrew reported. "There's a trench dug around the outer wall. It's about nine feet deep and about twenty-five feet wide, which adds an extra nine feet to the wall's height. The inner wall is heavily guarded by soldiers. The outer wall is barely guarded at all. In fact, we were able to easily slip out the gate of the outer wall the night we escaped."

Joshua's broad shoulders rose and fell with a sigh. His bright blue eyes showed a flicker of doubt. "Those are formidable fortifications."

Salmon felt as though they had failed Joshua. The only news they had to report was that Jericho was a strong, impenetrable fortress.

"To top it off," Andrew continued, "Jericho is ready for a lengthy siege. They just brought in the harvest, and they have many freshwater springs in the city. It could take many months, maybe even years to subdue the city."

"God will fight for us," Joshua said. "He always has."

Salmon wasn't so sure. Even with God's help, he didn't see how victory was possible. Joshua, tall and well built from the years of their journey through the wilderness and the many hardships they faced, turned and marched away toward the edge of the camp. He was withdrawing, Salmon knew, to meet with God as he did over every decision he made. His great uncle had a strong personality suited for leadership. He would call the people together once he and God determined the course of action. That could take hours or days.

Salmon decided to use the time to visit his family. His mother and father always offered a welcome reprieve from the pressures of attending Joshua. His parents loved God with all their hearts and lived every moment as though God were standing beside them. He wished his faith could be as strong as theirs.

As Salmon drew near to the family's tent, he expected his mother to come running out to meet him like she always did when he returned from missions, but she didn't.

Strange, Salmon thought.

He stopped outside the tent flap and listened. He could hear soft weeping.

"Mother!" He lifted the flap and stepped into the tent. "What's wrong?"

His mother, Jael, rose from her pallet and threw herself into Salmon's arms. His normally strong mother wilted against his body. He held her up, shrouding her in his protective embrace. He remained silent, knowing she would speak when she could.

Finally, Jael looked up at him, her liquid blue eyes puffy and red.

"He died, Salmon. Your father. He died." She broke into tears. She lowered herself onto her unmade pallet and put her face in her hands as sobs racked her body.

Salmon stared off into space, seeing nothing. What had happened? His father battled bad colds periodically, but otherwise, he was a very healthy man. Salmon sat on the pallet next to his mother and put his hand on her shoulder, hoping she could find the strength to explain.

"It was my fault," Jael whispered between sobs, almost too quiet for Salmon to hear. "I asked him to go out from our camp to gather some herbs for dinner. It was a bear. They found bear prints around his body. There were cub prints, too. The she-bear must have seen him as a threat."

Salmon couldn't think. He just sat, numb. How could God let this happen? He must have His reasons, yet Salmon couldn't keep from questioning God's motive.

He spent three days with his mother, Jael, soothing her with tea and broth when she refused to eat. He spoke with his father's brother, Ananiah, and arranged for him to take his mother into his tent until the wars were won and the people were settled in the

Promised Land. But his mother refused to leave her tent, the tent where all her memories were. He worried about her often and wanted to stay close in case he was needed, but he found himself having to leave her more and more, hoping she would be okay alone. He checked in on her as much as he could.

On the fourth day, Joshua called for an assembly. He stood before Israel, his red robe blowing in the wind, demanding attention, elation showing on his face. "We march against Jericho tomorrow!"

The people of God cheered. Joshua held up his hands to silence the congregation.

"God has given us a specific battle plan. He will show us that the battle truly is His. We are to march around Jericho for seven days. On the seventh day, we are to march around Jericho seven times, then God will tear down Jericho's defenses, and we will march on the city. It is very important that we not make any noise as we march. Only the trumpets will blow before the ark of God."

Salmon's ears perked up. They were taking the ark with them into battle? That didn't happen often.

"Once Jericho's walls are removed," Joshua continued, "we are to utterly destroy the city and all its inhabitants."

What about Rahab and her family? Salmon wondered. He'd have to talk to his uncle again about them and his promise to spare them.

"Every other city we have marched upon, God gave us the spoils to be our own. It will not be so with Jericho," Joshua said. "The spoils of Jericho are to be God's alone. Anyone who steals from God's spoils will be accursed. Leave the spoils of Jericho alone!

"Only one family of Jericho will be saved. Rahab, the harlot who hid our spies, has been promised safety. She will have a red cord fixed in her window. No one is to touch anyone in that house. Everyone and everything else in the city are to be destroyed completely!"

Rahab met Hagdad in the marketplace. She *had* to tell her about the coming attack.

"What will we do?" Hagdad asked. "I don't know if Levi will agree to come, but I'll try to persuade him. How can you even know for sure they're coming? Even if they do, how will they get through? I mean, Jericho is pretty well protected."

"I *don't* know. Not for sure," Rahab said. "But I'd rather be safe than sorry. My family is important enough that I'm willing to risk being made a fool of."

Hagdad looked deeply into Rahab's eyes. "I'll see what I can do." She sighed and moved off through the bustling streets.

Now for Emma, thought Rahab. She knew where the Aberstains used to live. She was glad Emma and her husband had gotten the house. It was a very nice place.

When Rahab arrived at Emma's house, she knocked loudly on the solid, rough door, hoping someone would answer. She glanced down at the potted flowers, pink roses, sitting on either side of the stoop. A smile played at the edges of Rahab's mouth.

Emma opened the door. Rahab saw her face fall. *She doesn't want to see me.*

"Rahab. How nice to see you." Her tone was dry and flat, yet Emma was as beautiful as always. Her long, dark hair was held back with a clip. Her face looked flushed, and she seemed to glow. Rahab took her little sister in, all the way down her rounded belly.

"Emma! When is your baby due?"

"In less than a month." Emma's answer was short and terse.

The tone of Emma's voice told Rahab that Emma believed all the awful things her father must be saying about her. She sighed, then groaned when she saw the rosewood baby cradle in the next room behind Emma. A knitted blanket hung over the side; small wooden carved toys sat on the floor in front of the cradle, arranged in order from smallest to largest.

"Emma, I have something very important to tell you." Rahab stopped. How much could she trust Emma with? What if Emma told? She'd have to tell Emma the story if she hoped to save her life. Rahab decided she'd have to put it all on the line.

Emma tapped her toe. "I'm listening." She crossed her arms in exasperation, clearly not happy to have Rahab standing on her doorstep.

"Israel is coming to destroy Jericho," Rahab said hurriedly. "You and your husband must come to my house if you wish to be safe."

"And what makes you think *your* house is any safer than anyone else's?"

"I have a promise of protection for anyone who is in my house when Israel attacks. A promise from Israel itself."

"You do know that it's treasonous to be talking about Jericho being overthrown—which is an impossibility," Emma snapped. "It's also treasonous to be close enough to Israel to receive promises of protection. I have to wonder how you have the gall to even show up at my house, never mind tell me all about all your sins. Get away from my house before my husband gets home. He *will* turn you in. And I might myself if you don't get off my property right now!"

Emma slammed the door in her face. Rahab raised her hand to knock again, then lowered it. She thought of Emma's baby, and tears filled her eyes. *Please let her change her mind.*

Rahab hurried back to her house to hug Lilly and hold her close. As she neared the inner wall, she saw Yassib leaning against her door. At the sound of her footsteps, he turned his head and straightened, weaving unsteadily on his feet.

"Rahab, what happened to your scarlet cord?" He asked. "Why isn't it wrapped around the pole? Are you no longer offering your services as a prostitute?"

Yassib's eyes were bleary, and he was still weaving. Clearly, he was drunk.

"No, Yassib, I'm not," Rahab replied. "I've decided harlotry is no longer for me."

"That's a shame, Rahab. Really it is. Why?"

"Go home, Yassib. You're drunk. And your wife wouldn't appreciate your talking to a harlot."

"C'mon, Rahab. Just one more time for good measure?" Yassib stumbled toward her, arms reaching out to embrace her.

"No, Yassib," Rahab said firmly. "Go home."

Yassib lurched toward her. Rahab backed away and quickly found herself in a corner, her back to the wall. Now what? She knew she couldn't fight Yassib. Even in his drunken state, he was stronger than she was and could easily subdue her.

"Looks like I got you right where I want you," Yassib sneered. "Now, give me some lovin'."

"Mama!" Lily called, sticking her head out the door of the house.

"Go back inside, Lily," Rahab said, trying to sound calm. "I'll be inside in a minute."

"It'll be longer than a minute," Yassib said, a look of pleasure on his face.

What will I do? God, if there is a God, help me!

Yassib reached out, tracing his hand from Rahab's shoulder down toward her breast. She stared defiantly into his face. Even if he forced her, she wouldn't let him enjoy her fear.

"Such a strong, unbroken spirit," Yassib said. "I would have enjoyed breaking you."

"Out of the way," Melham ordered gruffly, appearing beside Yassib in full soldier garb, breastplate on and sword at his side. "Rahab, I need to ask you a few questions."

Melham pushed past Yassib, took Rahab's elbow, and steered her toward her house. She breathed a sigh of relief. She didn't need to look back as she followed Melham up the steps to her front door. She knew from experience that Yassib's lusting eyes were following her.

Melham was all business, as usual, but something different stuck out to Rahab. The way he carried himself today, the way he walked, seemed to convey excitement about a secret only he knew.

"I know you helped the spies," Melham accused her once they were inside her house. "I *know* you did, but I don't have proof yet. When I do, I'll be back." He took a threatening step toward her. "If you're smart, you'll tell me the truth."

"I have only one thing to say to you, Melham." Though her insides were shaking, Rahab lifted her chin defiantly, "Get out of my house."

He blinked, startled, then he laughed. "I'll be back, harlot. You can be sure of that."

He stormed out of her house, slamming the door behind him. Rahab breathed a sigh of relief that he hadn't noticed the red cord hanging from the window. If Melham had seen it, if he'd taken it… no, she wouldn't think of that.

Instead, she knelt and drew Lily into a fiercely protective hug.

Chapter 13

The rams' horns sounded long and loud. Joshua was calling for an assembly. It was time for the soldiers to line up to march on Jericho. Normally, the five-and-one-half mile march would have seemed daunting, but their excitement made it seem like a short hike. The long unbroken tenor tone of the shofar continued to sound until all the soldiers were in place with swords in sheaths at their waist, helmets on, and shields slung over one arm. Everyone was ready.

Salmon watched as four Levites carried the Ark of the Covenant out of the tabernacle. The priests were clothed in fine white linen. Their linen bonnets sat snuggly upon their heads. Their white robes were long and flowing. The Ark sat upon their shoulders, held between them by two long golden poles. Salmon looked at the Ark, covered with a thick, heavy curtain of blue, purple and scarlet. On the curtain were many embroidered cherubs. Salmon would never get used to the beauty of the veil.

Seven other Levites took their place in front of the Ark, each bearing a shofar. They would blow them before the Ark of God in worship. The Levites would also use them to direct the battle.

The Levites blew a level note on their shofars, signaling the march would soon commence. Salmon could feel the excitement rippling through the ranks. A second signal blew, a low legato note, and the soldiers began to move forward as one man. *It begins.*

When the army reached the Jordan River, the water looked higher and swifter than it had when he and Andrew crossed it to spy on Jericho. How would they get across? Salmon's shoulders slumped. They were beaten before they'd even started. Surely, God knew they'd come up against this wall of water. Didn't He?

"Don't give up!" Joshua shouted, turning at the head of the column to face the soldiers. "God has brought us to the Jordan. He will see us safely across. We march forward!"

The Levites blew their trumpets, signaling the army to move forward once more. Instead of stopping at the water's edge, the Levites carrying the Ark stepped into the river. Suddenly the waters dried up, and the Levites were standing on dry ground. Salmon stared in awe. Again, God had shown Himself to be all-powerful. Who had he been to doubt? *I'm sorry, Lord.*

At Joshua's command, twelve men were chosen to collect twelve large rocks and build an altar to God in the middle of the river. The twelve rocks each represented one of the twelve tribes of Israel. Salmon watched as they placed rock upon rock. One man kept peering at the wall of water that stood high above him. The twelve soldiers were still standing on dry ground, but the waters of the Jordan kept piling up like waters before a dam. Soon, the altar was built, and the soldiers were able to move out of the river. Each of the twelve soldiers let out a visible sigh of relief. As soon as the whole army was clear of the Jordan, God allowed the waters to again flow freely. The mass of soldiers lifted their voices in praise to God. He truly was a great God worthy of all honor and praise.

The air in the inn seemed to be strangling her. Rahab had to get outside. She escaped to her rooftop, looked over the wall, and caught her breath.

In the distance, Rahab could see the Israelite army moving toward Jericho. *There must be half a million soldiers or more!* They moved as one person. It was a very intimidating sight. People on the street below, the one that ran along the top of the wall, were running to and fro in a frantic state. *Serves them right.* Now that Israel was coming, all her worries, even those surrounding Melham's visit, would be over.

Rahab went back inside with Lily and her servants, waiting for the attack to commence, hoping her family would join her. Surely, they'd remember!

"Please come," she said aloud to no one in particular.

Ira looked at her with questioning eyes.

"My family," she explained.

Gina reached out and took her hand. "I'm sure they'll make it in time." She sounded like a mother comforting her child, but Rahab didn't mind. She needed the comfort.

Rahab reached down and caressed Lily's face, pushing a stray lock of hair from her face. At least the one person she loved more than life itself was here and safe. Her little Lily Rose.

Because her house was on top of the wall, through the window where she'd hung her red cord, she could see the army of Israel drawing closer. As they watched, the soldiers turned toward the north and marched out of sight, following the wall. Perhaps the spies had found a weak spot in the wall in that direction and would attack from there. Within the next hour, Rahab saw Israel return to the front gate of Jericho, having completely circled the small city. Then the army turned and marched back toward the Jordan.

"Look, Mama! They're going away!" Lily pointed at the retreating army, a look of relief on her face.

"What is going on?" Gina asked, perplexed, moving forward to lean out the window. "Have they given up?"

"Surely they'll return," Rahab said, hoping it would be so. If Melham returned before the Israelite army… a shiver ran through her, and she pushed the thought away.

There was an eerie silence as Jericho stared in surprise that Israel was leaving. The silence turned to a murmur as people discussed what had just happened. Though the atmosphere seemed somewhat lighter, Rahab could still feel the fear and tension hanging in the air.

There came a quiet knock at the door. "Hello?" Rahab called through the heavy wooden beams of the door. She was being careful since Yassib had tried to attack her.

"Rahab, it's me," her mother replied, her voice muffled.

Rahab's hand went to her chest. Then she threw the door open wide.

"Mother! Hagdad!" They were both standing on her doorstep.

Hagdad's husband, Levi, stood behind them, wringing his hands. Next to him stood her brother, Aliyan, and her sister, Bilba. Rahab pushed past her mother and sister and pulled Aliyan into an embrace.

She'd missed so much of his life. Almost eight years had passed since she'd seen him last. She quickly did the math in her head. Aliyan was already thirteen years old!

Next, she stooped down and took Bilba in her embrace. Nine years old already? She closed her eyes, remembering the last time she had held Bilba. It had been the day long ago when she had left her in Hagdad's care to go inside and face her father. Rahab's eyes filled with tears. Little Bilba, not so little anymore.

Realizing she was being rude, Rahab sniffed back her tears, rose to her feet and turned to face her family.

Her mother was smiling a big, bright smile! The last time Rahab had seen her mother smile, she was six years old. And here it was again, bright and beautiful.

"Please, come in." Rahab swept her hand toward the door. Her family nodded and entered her house. Rahab was so excited. She was literally shaking. She could feel her smile stretching her face. It was almost painful, but she couldn't stop. Her family—at least part of it—had come. They'd be safe now. Rahab stepped inside, closed the door, and bolted it shut.

"Mother, how did you ever convince Father to let you come?"

"I didn't," she replied. "I've had enough of his abuse. I chose to come without him. I hope you're right, Rahab. If you're not, I have nowhere else to go."

"Nonsense." Rahab embraced her mother. "You will always have a home with me."

When had her meek, submissive mother gone from taking her father's abuse without question to this woman who stood up for herself? Rahab didn't know, but she liked the change.

Rahab looked around her. She saw Lily shyly standing in the shadows away from everyone else but close enough to hear the clamor.

"Come here, Sweetheart," Rahab waved at Lily to join her. "This is your meemaw. She's Mama's mother."

Lily's meemaw knelt down before her. "Hello, Honey."

Lily stood there staring at her, then finally took a step forward and gingerly placed her arms around her meemaw's neck. Rahab's mother pulled her into an embrace. Lily immediately stiffened up. Rahab knew Lily would grow to love her meemaw, but it would take time.

She wondered if Emma and her husband and her father would show up. Surely, they would.

For six more days, Rahab and her family watched Israel march around Jericho. The sound of thousands of sandals scraping on the rocky ground, the sound that made Jericho shiver in fear just days before, still reverberated against the city walls, but it no longer cast an eerie feeling upon Jericho. The people had gone from fearing Israel to mocking them.

They hung over the walls as far as they could and made fun of their apparently pointless march. If Israel hadn't found a way in yet, many said, they wouldn't find a way at all. They assumed Jericho would be safe. Rahab knew better, or at least, she hoped she did. Her faith was beginning to waver, though she didn't want to say so. She didn't want to frighten her mother.

On the seventh day, she watched as Israel again marched around Jericho just as they had done every other day, but today something was different. They didn't stop after their first time around the walls and march back toward their camp. They went around again.

The people of Jericho quieted, wondering what this meant. They moved back from the edges of the walls and watched in silence.

"They've gone around five times so far, Mama," Lily said, grabbing Rahab's hand.

Rahab looked down at Lily and smiled.

Rahab's mother knelt down in front of Lily. "You're such a good counter," she said.

Lily smiled broadly. "I could count since I was three," Lily boasted. "See, one, two, three, four, fi."

"They're going around *again*," Rahab exclaimed, surprised. "How long do you think they'll march?" she asked to no one in particular.

"Maybe today's the day," Ira suggested.

Everyone looked at Ira. She blushed and looked down at her feet.

"Maybe," Hagdad said.

Ira looked back up and smiled. She'd just been vindicated.

Salmon yawned again. He was so very tired. They'd marched around Jericho for six days now. The dust kicked up from the march choked him. His throat felt scratchy and raw. His legs ached, and his stomach growled.

When they reached the end of their march, Joshua turned to his troops. "Lift up your voices, Israel!" he called to them. "God has given us the city!"

Every soldier raised his voice in praise to God. They yelled as loudly as they could, Salmon among them, and over the crescendo of the voices, he began to hear a rumble and felt the earth tremble beneath his feet.

Rahab heard the Israelite trumpets blare and yelling so loud that it pierced her eardrums.

"Mama!" Lily cried, clinging to her skirt. "Mama, the noise is hurting my head!"

Rahab knelt down, drew her daughter into her arms, and pressed Lily's head against her shoulder. The floor beneath her feet groaned and shivered. Gina and Ira clung to each other. Her mother, Aliyan, Hagdad, and Levi held on to each other. Orbid stood with his feet spread wide apart, fists on his hips, swaying from side to side to stay upright on the shaking floor.

Rahab, with Lily holding to her skirt and rushing behind her, made her way to the window where the red cord was swinging like a pendulum. The floor was now rolling beneath her. She looked outside and saw the people clustered on the top of the wall holding onto each other and anything else they could grasp.

The walls seemed to be moving. Rahab clung to the bottom of the window, staring in disbelief as a crack appeared and slithered like a snake across the city wall. The people began to scream and run. A huge rumble drowned the blare of the trumpets, and a chunk of the wall broke and fell off. The walls were falling! Tumbling down with a roar like a thousand lions!

Dust billowed up, filling the air and pouring through the window. Coughing, Rahab slammed the shutters on all the windows, yet dust still seeped through the cracks. Rahab and Ira ran to the kitchen for cloths to put over their mouths and noses to block out some of the dust. They dampened the cloths and hurried back to the main room of the inn and handed them out to everyone so they could breathe easier.

A sharp knock sounded at the door. Rahab opened it and stared at Yassib standing on her doorstep. What was he doing here? Had someone told him her house was safe?

Rahab gasped. Her father must have told his great friend.

"Let me in," Yassib growled, trying to push past her.

"No!" Rahab cried, shoving the door with every bit of strength she possessed.

Yassib pushed back, the door inching forward, then Orbid was there, her mother beside him. Her manservant was taller and much stronger than Yassib. He braced his hands on the door, so did her mother, and the heavy wooden portal swung shut in Yassib's face. Aliyan appeared and quickly barred the door.

"That *pig* is not coming in here!" her mother declared fiercely. "I *know* he's the reason you ran off to the temple. He came to my home and gloated to your father about using and abusing you, all in the name of worship, while you were at the temple. I heard them talking. Yassib *deserves* to die for what he did to you!"

Rahab put her arms around her mother and hugged her. She couldn't argue. It was true. He *did* deserve to die.

When another knock came at the door, her mother cried out, "Don't let him in, Rahab!"

"What if it's not Yassib?" Rahab lifted the piece of wood that barred the door and jerked it open.

Her father pushed his way into the house. Over his shoulder Rahab caught a glimpse of the streets below, people screaming and running, and bright flashes of metal—swords, she realized, sweeping the air over their heads, then her father slammed the door shut, snatched the bar from her, and dropped it into place. He turned to face her, his face pale, his eyes open wide.

"I was walking through town and saw the soldiers coming," he said, his voice quavering. "This was the closest place to hide. It has *nothing* to do with your warning." But Rahab knew it had. Why else would he have been so close by?

Her father hung his head, looking at his shoes, then looked over Rahab's shoulder.

"Okay, okay," he replied. "I heeded your warning. I'm here. Now to see if we will truly be safe." He paused, then peeked up at her face. "Thank you," he said quietly.

Rahab smiled. Her father had humbled himself enough to thank her. Maybe he was starting to change into the man she had always wished her father would be.

Rahab was jerked back to the present as Lily pushed her frail body into Rahab's side, fear evident on her face. Rahab tried to keep her mask of confident bravery in place.

She could still hear the sounds from outside through the door: screams, wailing, the clang of swords and armor. Rahab's knees felt weak and shaky. She prayed the spies would remember their promise. Would they be saved? Or would they be forgotten?

Salmon had watched in awe as the walls of Jericho fell, tumbling forward and filling the moat that was dug around the outside wall. The inner wall fell even with it, butting up against it. The roar of so many tons of rock collapsing had nearly deafened him, and the dust that spewed up had nearly blinded him.

He was still batting it away when suddenly, supernaturally, the dust cleared around him and his fellow soldiers. Inside the fallen walls of Jericho the dust still hung in a heavy pall. He could see that the fallen walls had made a bridge into the city. All the army had to do was march across it.

The priests again blew their trumpets, not in the sounds of worship, but in a sharp staccato note directing the army forward into the city. It was time to take Jericho.

Salmon felt a hand on his shoulder. He turned to see Joshua.

"Go, my nephew," he said, his face and his beard brown with dust. "Save the harlot who hid you and Andrew as you promised. Leave her and her family outside our camp. It's against God's laws to let heathens enter the camp."

"Yes, Uncle," Salmon replied, and Andrew, standing next to him, nodded.

Salmon and Andrew wove their way across the bridge of fallen walls and through the city. Only one part of the wall still stood—the portion of wall upon which stood Rahab's house. He and Andrew exchanged a look of amazement.

"God is great," Andrew said.

"His wonders never cease," Salmon replied.

Quickly, they climbed the stairs to the top of the wall, taking them two at a time. When they reached the door, they pushed at it, but it wouldn't give. Salmon drew his sword and banged the hilt against the heavy wood. He heard women scream in terror.

"Open up!" he shouted. "It's Salmon!"

Rahab yanked the door open. Her hair and her robe were covered with dust. She blinked at him, and an audible sigh of relief escaped her lips. "I thought you'd forgotten about us!"

She looked like she wanted to hug him. Salmon took a step back.

"God wouldn't let me forget my promise," he assured her.

"Then I thank your God," Rahab said, bowing her head, "for saving my family."

"Hurry now." Andrew urged her. "We must be quick."

Rahab and her family followed Salmon and Andrew as they led them out of the house and through the streets of Jericho. The packs Rahab had prepared for her and Lily weighed heavily upon her shoulders. Masses of dead people lay everywhere: children, parents, grandparents.

Rahab pulled Lily close and covered her eyes with her free hand so she couldn't see the carnage. Rahab tried not to look at the dead bodies, but she was acutely aware that they were there. The stench of blood and death made her gag. The dust in the air was starting to clear, carried away by the breeze. She still heard the sounds of killing all around her, etching itself into the deepest recesses of her mind.

She caught sight of a fallen and familiar figure from the corner of her eye. She looked; she couldn't help herself. There, lying in a pool of blood, lay Yassib. A smile played on the edges of her lips. Rahab laughed to herself. She knew she shouldn't revel in the death of another, but gratefulness welled up inside of her. He had finally gotten what he deserved.

Salmon and Andrew led them over the bridge of fallen walls toward the Jordan and the camp of Israel. The wall wasn't difficult to walk on. The rocks had been smoothed when the wall was built. Yet Rahab tripped many times on her way, the shock of what had happened turned her legs stiff and her feet clumsy. Within sight of the Israelite camp, Salmon and Andrew drew them to a halt.

"You must stay here," Salmon said gravely to Rahab. "Joshua instructed us that you are not to enter the camp."

"What are we to do?" Rahab asked.

"Wait," Salmon said and turned away with Andrew to make the five-and-a-half-mile trek back to Jericho.

Chapter 14

Rahab put Lily down. Although she was much too big to be carried, Rahab had managed to carry her on her back for part of the trip. The trek had been too much for her.

Rahab looked behind her. She could see smoke rising above Jericho. Israel was burning the city. Her heart clenched. Jericho had been her home for twenty-four years, and now it was gone.

All she could see in every direction was vast and empty wilderness. The sand seemed to stretch as far as her eyes could see, unlike Jericho which had plenty of scraggily grass lush with wildflowers and herbs. A few lonely palms, scattered here and there, guarded what little bit of water they could hoard. A solitary hawk glided sleekly through the sky, riding the soft breeze. The breeze tussled a few loose strands of Rahab's hair, making it tickle her face.

She turned again and looked at the Israelite camp, a sea of tents, with no end in sight. She was surprised by the size of the tents. They were large enough to accommodate whole families. They appeared to be made of large blankets of goatskin.

The women of the camp were about their daily chores. Some sat before large looms, weaving goat hair into strips. Some were repairing their tents. Others were keeping a wary eye on the children that stood at the edge of the camp staring curiously at Rahab and her family.

Open cooking fires flickered in the heat. Goats, asses, and cattle roamed between the tents and around the camp munching on sparse clumps of grass that sprang up here and there. She could hear the rush of the Jordan River and the buzzing of the flies that swarmed around the animals.

The smell of dust had faded as they had moved further from Jericho and was replaced with the sweet scent of an oncoming rain that wrapped itself around her. Finally, the children went back to playing, their happy laughter drifting to her on the wings of the slight breeze.

"What now?" Alyian asked.

Rahab turned toward her brother. "Salmon said to wait."

"Indeed," Hagdad said. "Wait for what?"

"I don't know," Rahab replied, taking Lily's hand.

She led her daughter and her family toward the thin shade beneath a close palm tree. Lily sank down at the base and curled into a ball, exhausted. Rahab leaned against a boulder near the palm and sighed. What *was* next?

She looked back again toward Jericho. She thought she wouldn't care, that she would be happy that the men of the city were finally punished. Remembering the carnage, the dead lying everywhere, she shivered. As much as she hated to admit it, she would miss Jericho. Her city, her home, was gone. Forever.

"We can't stay here," Rahab's father stated as a matter of fact, a glare in his eyes. "We need to find another city to settle in. There are a few around here. We can have our choice. Gilgal is closest. Yes, we'll go to Gilgal."

Everyone nodded in agreement. Everyone but Rahab.

"I'm staying," she said.

"Staying? Why?" asked Levi, eyes open wide. "There's no place to bed down. They won't let you in their camp."

"I have no other choice. I *need* to learn more about their God. The Deliverer of Israel. The Provider. The One who kept them safe and cared for them for over forty years. The One that can knock two walls down flat, leaving just one section standing just because of a promise made by one of His servants."

Rahab's mother moved toward Rahab and grasped her by the shoulders. "No. Rahab, you can't leave again! I just got you back! I can't. I won't let you go again. Please, Rahab."

Her mother pulled her into a strong embrace and held on with all she had. She held her as if she let go the ground would open up and swallow Rahab whole. Her body shook with sobs.

"Leave her alone, woman." Her father crossed his arms and glared; his eyes boring into her mother's back. "It's her choice. It's a foolish one, but it's hers all the same."

"You're right. It is my choice," Rahab declared. "And it's what I choose."

"If she's staying, so am I." Rahab's mother loosened her embrace just a little. "I will not lose you again."

"We'll leave in the morning at first light." Her father huffed, ignoring his wife and Rahab. "Find a comfortable place to lie down and get some sleep."

He sank to the ground, his arms folded across his chest, apparently not happy in the least.

Everyone else followed suit using the small packs they had brought for pillows. Rahab sat on the ground, her back to the boulder. She watched as everyone quickly fell asleep, worn out emotionally and physically from the excitement of the day.

She wasn't able to fall asleep in the twilight. She thought of all she had done with her life. Caring for her siblings. Taking her father's wrath in stride, not allowing him to crush her spirit like he had done to her mother. Yassib. That was a whole saga of its own. Starting her own business. Playing the harlot. Helping the spies. Saving part of her family. She thought of Emma, tears blurring her eyes. If only she had come.

Night fell quickly. She glanced around, not really looking at anything. Stars twinkled the night sky, dancing to their own symphony. The crescent moon peeked out from behind the clouds, giving off a little light. Bats flew around above her, catching the nighttime bugs. There were a few palms silhouetted in the darkness. A small animal skittered across the sand about twenty feet away. *Probably a shrew*, she figured by its movements. She heard the howl of a gray wolf, thankfully far away. She took a deep breath and settled against the rock.

She knew why sleep alluded her. Her body was used to being up most of the night entertaining male customers and sleeping half of the day. Her body would have to get used to the changes now that her life was different. It would be a difficult transition. Oh well, if she couldn't sleep, at least she could rest.

Do I really want to stay? It was a big decision. It would mean leaving her family—and she had just gotten them back. Plus, the Israelites might never let her into their camp.

What would she do then?

Jericho had fallen quicker than Salmon had thought possible. God had fought for them as He promised. He felt a hand on his shoulder and turned to see Andrew standing behind him.

"You did well today," Andrew said.

Salmon nodded slowly. This was his first battle. He'd never seen so much blood and gore. He felt squeamish as he looked at the dead bodies all around him. He had done that. He had killed today. He started to feel dizzy.

"Are you alright?" Andrew reached out with both hands and gripped Salmon's shoulders. "You don't look so good."

Salmon made himself breathe slowly, swallowing the bile in his throat. Finally, he nodded again. "I'll be okay."

"I didn't do well with my first battle either," Andrew said. "It's one thing to hear about war. It's much harder to fight one. It will get easier. Tell God how you feel. It will help."

The soft breeze changed directions. It carried the strong scent of death. Salmon's stomach clenched. He tried to talk himself through the nausea, but it was too late. He wheeled away from Andrew and wretched.

Andrew patted his back softly. "It will be okay."

Finally finished, Salmon rubbed his mouth with the back of his hand, stooped and picked up some sand and rubbed it between his hands. He stood up tall again and tried to regain his composure. *Breathe through your mouth.*

The next morning greeted Rahab. The sun's warm rays wrapped themselves around her, easing some of the tension in her shoulders. She sat up and stretched. She smiled as she looked around at her family, still sleeping peacefully.

Lily was snuggled against Rahab, her head in her lap. She had fallen asleep when Rahab was still sitting up. She hadn't had the heart to wake her when she finally scooted down to sleep. She reached down and caressed Lily's braids. She sighed in contentment as she studied her daughter's face. So blessed.

Then she remembered. Remembered the horror they had gone through the day before. She felt tears well up in her eyes. The children. The women. They had died, too. She tried to block out the images, but they seemed to be imprinted in her consciousness. She buried her face in her hands, trying to think of the new day and imagining what might happen to her today.

Her mother stirred and sat up slowly. She rubbed her neck and shoulders, trying to work the kinks out. "I'm so sore from sleeping on the ground," she said.

Everyone else woke up and began milling around their temporary camp. Rahab's stomach growled, reminding her she hadn't eaten since the mid-day meal.

She heard the shuffling of footsteps and looked toward the Israelite camp. Two women walked toward them with big bowls, a pitcher, and wrapped packages in their hands.

"We brought you some food," one of the women said. "We thought you might be hungry."

Rahab was grateful. She smiled wide. "Thank you, kindly."

Aliyan jumped to his feet. He had been sitting next to the boulder. He rushed toward them and reached out to accept the food. "Thank you so much," he said. "Let me help you."

The ladies, who ignored Aliyan's offer, were both clothed in long brown and white robes and leather sandals, the straps wrapping around their legs and reaching up to their knees. They spread a rough cloth on the sand and set the bowls on the ground.

The first woman pointed toward the large pitcher. "Goat's milk," she said and pointed toward the bowl. "Cheese." The second woman held the wrapped parcels and laid them on the cloth. "Bread and grapes."

Aliyan nodded in gratitude as he looked at the packages. "Thank you."

The women, not impressed, turned and walked back to the camp, taking their sour faces and rigid, uncomfortable stance with them.

Rahab rubbed Lily's back, her normal way of waking her up. Lily stirred. Rahab knew Lily's body would be heavy with sleep. Lily had never been much of a morning person, and today was no different.

"Come on, Honey. Time to wake up." Lily slowly sat up and rubbed her eyes with both fists, moving enough to lean heavily into Rahab's shoulder. Rahab used both hands to sit Lily up and moved toward the blanket. She knelt on the edge of the cloth, unwrapped the packages and motioned Lily over to her. She placed a chunk of bread, some cheese and a few grapes in front of her.

"Eat up," she said to Lily and passed the food to the rest of her family.

"Then we must begin our trek to Gilgal," her father said. He looked pointedly at Rahab.

Rahab sighed. He still expected her to follow him. How could she make him understand that she was staying and why she had to stay? Would he accept what she said? Or would he disown her again, this time for turning her back on her family and their god, Astarte?

Salmon bent over to fill the large pitcher with water. He had been up for two hours, busying himself with chores. Why had his father died? He began to wonder if God cared. He had taken his father and left her mother bereft. *No. I can't think like that!* He shook his head, trying to make the blasphemous thoughts go away, but they remained, digging deep talons into the dark recesses of his mind.

"How do you feel today?" Andrew asked from behind him.

"I'm all right," Salmon lied. He was still shaken and hadn't slept at all last night. Horrid, graphic nightmares and the images of the blood and death would not let go of him.

"Are you sure? You look a little pale."

Salmon nodded, refusing to look at Andrew. "I'm fine." This time he said it more forcefully and with more confidence.

Andrew raised an eyebrow, shrugged, and walked away. Salmon *would* be fine. He just had to convince himself.

Chapter 15

"I'm ready to go," Rahab's father said gruffly.

Everyone rose to their feet, even Rahab. Then she realized she was following his orders, as she had always done. *I am a grown woman*, she reminded herself and leaned against the boulder, her arms folded across her chest.

"I said, 'I'm ready to go!'" Her father barked, glaring pointedly at Rahab.

"And I said, 'I'm not going.'" She straightened her stance and glared right back at him.

Her mother stared at Rahab, her eyes wide, jaw hanging open. She gathered her composure and said quietly, "I'm staying with Rahab."

"What?" Her father asked in a loud voice. He glared at his wife and took an aggressive step toward her.

Rahab jumped in between her parents. "She's not going, Father. She said she's staying. You're not going to abuse her into submission. Not now. Not ever again."

Her father's eyes narrowed, and he set his jaw. Then he turned on his heel. "C'mon," he growled to everyone else. "We're leaving *now*."

"Bilba's not going either." Debra looked down at her nine-year-old, pulling her into her side.

Rahab's father humphed and glared at his wife. He threw his arms down to his side. "Looks like I don't have a say." He snapped. "Anything else I should know?"

Rahab looked at Gina and Ira. Their downcast faces, the tears in their eyes told Rahab everything she needed to know. They were going with her father too. Rahab pulled them both into an embrace. "I'm going to miss you terribly," she said.

"We're going to miss you too," Gina spoke into her hair. She pulled back to look at Rahab. She smiled, her lips barely curving. "You'll do fine," Gina said.

"And so will you," Rahab replied.

Ira stood looking at Rahab, tears in her eyes. "We'll see each other again. We will," but she didn't look too sure of herself. Then she and Gina turned and slowly walked away, arm in arm.

Rahab's mother looked at Aliyan, a plea in her eyes.

Aliyan lowered his eyes. "I'm going with father."

Her mother slumped. She would be losing her son. Rahab knew why Aliyan was joining him. He had always put other people's feeling before his own, even as a little child. Rahab may have done the same in his place. Her father, Jerishium, needed someone. As his only son, Aliyan must have believed that to be his responsibility.

Rahab's father turned to go, Hagdad and Levi following him. Hagdad looked backward at Rahab. Her eyes were large and pleading, but Rahab had made her decision. She was staying whether her father liked it or not.

Rahab's mother took a step forward and reached out her hand to take Aliyan's and pulled him into a long, warm embrace, tears flowing down her cheeks.

Aliyan finally pulled back. Staring into his mother's eyes, he reached out and rubbed her arms. "Mother, I..." He looked over her shoulder into the desert. "I love you," he whispered as tears began to trail down his cheeks. "I love you," he said again.

Stepping past his mother, he grasped Rahab and pulled her into his arms. He nuzzled his face into her braided hair and squeezed harder. Rahab reached up, stroking the back of his head. He stepped back and looked into her eyes.

Aliyan knelt down in front of Bilba, his little sister, and reached out to chuck her chin. "You be good," he said. "Take good care of mother." After pulling her into a warm embrace, he stood up, straight and tall, then he turned to catch up with his father.

Her mother's hand came up to her mouth, trying to stifle the sobs rising in her throat. "I wish..." Her mother began, but she didn't finish her sentence. Rahab understood. She had made a decision to leave her family behind many years ago, just as her mother was doing now.

Rahab put her arms around her mother and pulled her close. She laid her head on Rahab's shoulder and cried. Rahab stroked her hair.

"Is Meemaw okay?" Lily whispered, her voice trembling with sympathetic tears.

"She will be," Rahab said, smiling at her daughter.

"I'll miss Aliyan dearly," her mother choked out, pulling away from Rahab and crossing her arms. "I wish he had stayed, too."

"I know," Rahab said. She looked down at Lily and Bilba and took their hands. She could only imagine how it must feel to watch her children walk away. Possibly forever. She felt deeply for her mother.

Her mother's tears stopped as they sat watching Lily play, wondering what to do next. Wondering if Israel would accept them.

"Why are you still here?" someone asked from behind them.

Rahab spun around to face the voice. Andrew. It was midday, and she still hadn't gotten her nerve up to ask the Israelites if she could stay with them.

Rahab and her mother stared at Andrew. Here was an opportunity to make her case, and Rahab couldn't find her voice. She couldn't even form words in her mind.

Andrew leaned against the boulder. Her boulder. She knew it was silly to lay claim to a boulder, but it was the only thing she had. It was her firm foundation—the only thing that kept her from running scared. She didn't know why, but she had always looked for something—anything—to ground her.

"Why are you still here?" Andrew repeated the question.

"I don't want to leave." Rahab immediately shrunk back. *That was stupid. He knows that already!* "I—we want to ask if we can stay. I want to learn more about your God. He seems so wonderful. He has cared for Israel even when no one else did. I've heard stories, so many stories, and your God is the center of them all. He cares about you, for you. I want to know a God that loves His children so. A God that loves a harlot and saved her from death. I want to stay."

Rahab pressed her lips together. There. She had said it. It was out there. She waited nervously for his answer. If he said no, maybe they could still catch up to her family.

"Stay here," Andrew said and then he turned and walked back to the Israelite camp.

Stay here. *Hmph.* Rahab crossed her arms and waited. It wasn't long before Andrew returned with another man at his side.

"This is Joshua," Andrew said.

Joshua was about the same height as Andrew, but he carried with him an air of authority. His dark hair was cut short. His eyes were deep-set and sparkling blue like sapphires. His hands, calloused from hard work, hung at his sides. Could this be *the* Joshua? The one Rahab had heard about? The one who had taken Moses' place? The leader of Israel? Why was he bothering with her, a horrible person, a harlot?

Joshua stood straight and tall, his eyes narrowing as he studied her face. Rahab suddenly felt very self-conscious.

"Why do you want to stay?" he asked her.

She took a deep breath. "I want to learn more about your God, the God Who saved a harlot and her family because of a promise made by one of His servants. I want to accept Him as my God. I want your God to be my God."

"And you?" He turned to look at Rahab's mother.

"I want to be with my daughter and my granddaughter. I know that's not the answer you want to hear, but that is my reason. But if your God is so very wonderful, I'd like to hear about Him too."

Rahab smiled at her mother. She noticed her mother was nervously wringing her hands, the very same nervous action that Rahab often found herself doing.

Joshua slowly nodded his head and then looked at Andrew, a smile vying for the all-business look on his face. "Take them into the camp. Have the women clothe them appropriately, and then take them to Salmon. He'll see to their training."

Andrew looked Rahab over for a moment before nodding his head. "Yes, sir."

"They can live with Dorri," Joshua said. "Dorri needs someone. Dorri has a desire to serve and can love anyone. She'll welcome Rahab and her mother."

Andrew turned and walked toward the camp. Rahab and her mother, holding Lily's hands between them, followed.

Get them appropriately clothed? Rahab looked down at her clothes, the clothing of a harlot. The bright colors—red, blue, and purple—screamed "Look at me!" Her neckline dipped low, giving an embarrassing view of her bosom. Her robe was open in the back, showing as much of her skin as was possible without the robe falling off. It was pulled tightly around her, clinging to every curve. Large gold earrings hung from her ears. Her hair was pulled up in seductive braids, which fell gracefully over her right shoulder. Her clothing was definitely different from the rough, long, and modest garments of the Israelite women.

Her mother was more modestly clothed, but her robe still showed off more of her body than those of the Israelites did. The green garment hung loosely on her mother and reached to the ground, but it exposed her shoulders. The garments of the Israelite woman seemed to cover every part of their body.

As Rahab, Lily, Bilba, and her mother followed Andrew through the camp, people turned to look at the odd caravan, their curious eyes following them as they moved through the midst of them. Finally, Andrew stopped in front of a tent.

"My wife, Terrah, will help you find suitable garments." He waved his hand toward the tent, motioning for them to enter.

Sitting in the rear of the tent, Terrah looked up at the sound of people entering. She smiled when she saw her guests. Her smile was genuine, lighting up her entire face, reaching from her lush, turned up lips and up to her bright blue eyes. Her black hair was long, reaching down to her waist, almost brushing the floor. The deep waves in her hair were beautiful, making it difficult for Rahab to look away. Terrah's white robe rustled around her as she slowly stood up and came toward them. Her red sash was tied loosely above her rounded belly. She looked to be about six months pregnant.

"It's nice to meet you," Terrah said, her arms out and pulling Rahab into a hug.

Rahab was surprised by the hug but awkwardly accepted it, wrapping her arms around her and then quickly stepping back.

"It's nice to meet you, too," she said politely.

"Terrah, Joshua asks that you find clothes for these ladies. This is Rahab, her daughter Lily, and her mother…" Andrew paused, his hand raised, staring at her.

Rahab realized she hadn't introduced her family. "Debra," she offered, "and my sister, Bilba."

"Debra and Bilba," he repeated, and then he turned and left.

Terrah helped them dress in the new clothing and then gave them a basin of water and a clean towel. "This is to wash your face."

Rahab could only imagine what she looked like. She had painted her face—light color above her eyes, her upper and lower lashes outlined in kohl and her lips painted dark—the morning that Jericho was taken. After two days of stress and tears, mixed with all the dust and grime of the trek out of the city to the Israelite camp, she was sure she was a sight to behold.

Even clothed in Israelite garments, which were long and flowing and made of a drab brown, Rahab, Debra, Bilba, and Lily would always stick out among them. Their skin was much darker than that of the Israelites' olive colored skin, and their dark hair demanded tight braids, otherwise, it kinked and frizzed around their faces.

Once they were modestly dressed, Andrew returned and again led them through the camp. Rahab saw Salmon in the distance. He was gathering pieces of wood from the ground.

"Salmon!" Andrew called to him. "Joshua has a task for you."

Salmon jerked up at the sound of Andrew's voice. He hadn't seen anyone approach. His face felt hot from the tears he had let flow freely just moments prior. He knew Andrew could see the trails left behind. Surely, he would understand.

Salmon's gaze shifted toward Rahab. She wasn't as tall as he remembered. Her black hair was starting to frizz out of its previously tight braids. Her face looked downcast and humbled compared to the proud, haughty woman he had met days earlier. She was wearing clothes that drew one's gaze to her face instead of the revealing clothing she had worn before. He was sure his surprise showed at the transformation.

"What task does Joshua have for me?" Salmon asked.

"He wants you to train Rahab and her daughter, Lily, and her mother, Debra, and her daughter, Bilba in the ways of God."

Train her? *A* harlot? *Surely there must be some mistake.* Salmon didn't want anything to do with this woman. He would go to his great uncle, Joshua, as soon as he could and get this straightened out.

Andrew nodded to the four women, turned and left. Salmon dropped his bundle of sticks and hurried toward Joshua's tent. He had to get this righted. Rahab, her mother, and the girls followed along behind him, clearly uncertain about what they were supposed to do.

When he reached Joshua's tent, he threw back the flap, took a deep breath, and stepped inside.

Joshua stood over a small table studying a map of Canaan that they had acquired along the way. "Yes, Salmon?" Joshua asked. "What can I do for you?"

"Andrew said I'm to train the harlot in the ways of God." He rubbed his face with both hands, trying to wipe the tear stains away. "I can't do this, Joshua. I just can't do this."

Joshua looked at Salmon for a moment then ran his hand over his newly shorn hair. Salmon *had* noticed that Joshua's hair was getting a little long.

"I think it will be good for you, Salmon. You need something to take your mind off your troubles. Doing something for someone else will help you to heal."

Salmon stared at Joshua. Surely he hadn't heard what he just had. *Heal?* He didn't need to heal. He needed his father back. "But Joshua, I can't. I just—"

Joshua held up his hand, and Salmon fell silent. "It has been decided, Salmon. Despite your rebuttals, Rahab, her little girl, her mother, and her sister are your pupils. You are to teach them the ways of God. And you *will* teach them. You don't have to like it. But you *will* do it."

Salmon clenched his jaw. He didn't dare gainsay Joshua, but he wanted to. He was furious, livid at having a harlot foisted on him.

"Explain to Rahab that you will be instructing her and her family in the ways of our God," Joshua continued. "Then escort them to Dorri's tent. I've spoken with her, and she is happy to give the newcomers a home."

He glared at his great uncle a moment longer, then nodded curtly and stormed out of his tent. As he stalked away from Joshua's tent, Salmon realized that

Rahab, her mother—*what had Andrew said her name was?*—Debra, Bilba, and Lily were following him once more.

Might as well start now, he thought angrily. The sooner they're trained, the sooner I can be done with them.

"I'm so happy you will be staying with me! We'll have such a great time!" Dorri said. Her sentences tumbled out fast and bumping into each other. Rahab wondered when their hostess would stop to take a breath. "Do you know how long you'll be staying with me? I hope it will be for a *very* long time! I love company. You can sleep on the kids' old pallets. They moved out years ago, but I couldn't bring myself to get rid of them. In fact, I have them set in the exact same places they have always been." Dorri seemed very sweet and eager to please. The way she prattled on made Rahab believe that she was a very lonely person. Joshua was right. She needed someone.

Rahab looked over her new friend. Her tight curls, black with a touch of gray around the temples, were a little longer than shoulder length. She was short, maybe four feet eight, and a little plumper than the other women she'd seen in the camp. Her eyes were bright and cheerful. Her dimpled cheeks were rounded and rosy. Her robe, yellow with a purple sash—extravagant, matching her personality—was a little tight on her full bust and plump body. She wasn't wearing any sandals; her toes peeked out from beneath her robe. She was a cheerful person, full of joy, the kind of person that never stopped smiling.

Rahab soon learned that Dorri's young husband had died almost twenty years ago. After his death, she was forced to marry his brother, a man she knew nothing about. They had to marry according to Israelite law, but they didn't have to like it. They made an arrangement: she left him alone, and he left her alone. She'd poured her life into her only daughter. Her two sons had already grown into young men and had ventured out to build lives of their own.

Since her daughter married a man from the tribe of Dan a little over eight years ago, Dorri had been completely alone. Her second husband, once her brother in law, had died in battle six months ago and she was too old to marry again. Her daughter and son in law lived on the far side of the Israelite camp, making it hard for them to visit. Dorri had been lost since.

Rahab soon realized Dorri was using her and her little family to fill the void in her life. And who was she to argue? They needed someone, and Dorri was the perfect fit. Dorri and her mother got along well, chatting and cooking and weaving. They quickly began to function as a family unit and fell into an easy routine. Rahab was hopeful that this arrangement would work out well for all of them.

Two weeks later, Rahab, Debra, Lily, and Bilba left Dorri's tent to meet Salmon at their usual spot near the edge of the camp for a new lesson, but Salmon was nowhere to be seen. Again. They sat under a lone palm tree, waiting. The sun's heat was lessened by the little shade it gave.

When Rahab heard a rustle behind her, she turned and saw Salmon coming toward them, a gloating look on his face. Her anger flared. She tried to put up with Salmon being late and rushing them through lessons, but two weeks had passed, and she'd had enough.

"Where have you been?" Rahab pushed to her feet, fists straight down at her sides, her face flushed. "You're late again."

Salmon stood there with a stupid grin on his face, obviously enjoying her irritation. He might not care about the lessons, but she did.

"And why do you rush through the lessons?" Rahab put her hands on her hips. "I want to learn everything I can about God, but you spend only a few minutes at a time with us. You aren't teaching us a thing!"

"I'm doing this because Joshua ordered me to, not because I want to," Salmon said bluntly, his jaw tight. "If you don't like my teaching, then take it up with my great uncle."

With that, he turned on his heel and marched away. Rahab resisted the urge to throw a rock at his head. Debra laughed.

It was nice to hear her laugh, but now was not the time. Rahab glared at her mother.

"Why are you laughing, Mother? I don't see anything funny about this."

"I just can't help seeing how perfect you and Salmon are for each other."

Rahab's made a disgusted frown. "Mother! I can't believe you! I don't want anything to do with *any* man. Especially *him*!"

"You'll change your mind." Her mother patted her on the shoulder, a sly look on her face. "You'll see."

Chapter 16

Rahab's angry flare made Salmon more determined than ever to make her life miserable. He continued to rush through lessons, and she continued to look like she wanted to kill him. He was short and curt with her, just like any harlot deserved.

But Lily... Lily deserved happiness. It wasn't her fault that her mother was a harlot. Lily made Salmon smile, and she deserved his smiles. She was a precious girl. Reluctantly, Salmon decided he should at least try to be civil to Rahab for Lily's sake. Rahab *was* her mother, after all.

The next day, before he began the lesson, while Lily and Bilba played and Debra watched them, Salmon drew Rahab off to the side. "I'm sorry," he said gruffly, "that I've been so rough with you."

"I don't need an apology from you," Rahab retorted. "I need you to teach me."

Her voice was cold, but there was fire in her dark eyes. She turned away from him and clapped her hands. "Come, Lily. Come, Bilba. It's time for our lesson."

Salmon was speechless. He'd apologized, and she'd rebuffed him. If Joshua were here, he could imagine what his uncle would say: "What do you expect after the way you've treated her?" Salmon felt ashamed,

shamed by a *harlot* and his sudden realization that he'd been using Rahab to vent the anger he felt over his father's death.

The children scampered to Rahab's side. Her mother joined them, and the four of them settled onto the sand beneath the palm tree where they met for their lessons. Salmon dropped to his heels in front of them and withdrew a scroll from the folds of his robe.

"Today, we're going to learn about God's creation," he said, unrolling the scroll. "Moses penned it down for us."

"But Salmon," Lily said in her sweet voice. "We studied that last time."

"Creation testifies of God. Everything—all that we see and hear, everything we touch—everything testifies of God," Salmon said. "If they had voices, the rocks, the sand, and the sun would praise Him out loud. Watermelons always have an even number of seeds. Beans *all* grow to the right. Day comes every morning. Dark comes every night. Everything we look at, everything we see, proves there is a God who loves and cares for us and created this world for us."

He closed the scroll and stood up. Rahab rose to her feet with him. Salmon gave her a curt nod and turned to walk away.

"That's it?" Rahab snapped behind him. "That's the whole lesson?"

Salmon turned and saw her glare at him, her fists planted on her hips.

"Joshua said I have to train you," he replied in a flat, hard voice. "He did not say how long the lessons had to be. I'm done for today."

Rahab opened her mouth—to rail at him, Salmon was sure—then she closed it, and reached her hands down to the children.

"Lily, Bilba. Come," she said. The children sprang up and took her hands. "Good day."

She barely nodded to him, turned and swept the children away toward the camp. Her mother rose, shook her head at Salmon with an amused expression on her face, and followed her daughter.

Early the next morning, Rahab left Dorri's tent to draw their daily water. She paused to balance the jar on her hip, took a deep breath, and looked around her.

Everything looked different to her and had for a while, now that she was seeing through the eyes of faith. She saw the small bunches of grass, the sand, the palm trees as a creation of the Almighty God. The breeze, once simply a wonderful thing on hot days, was more than something she was thankful for. It was a blessing sent from God.

The birds that flew above her were a miracle. God had somehow made their dense bodies to fly. Lily, her wonderful blessing, had become something she thanked God for every day. Her life, which she'd taken for granted, became a gift from God. She took another deep breath and let it out in a sigh of contentment. God was great!

She thought about how much she had changed in the weeks since she had come to Israel. She'd worked so hard to change the way she walked from the seductive sway she's learned in the temple of Astarte. She'd also changed her way of speech from the breathy murmur taught by the priestesses to be soft and smooth like that of the Israelite women around her.

She had grown used to the hot, confining garments. Her work ethic had improved. Once she'd had servants to do all her work so she could focus on harlotry. Now she shouldered her share of the housekeeping chores. At first, her muscles were soft, now she was strong and capable. She had changed in so many ways.

The more she learned about God, the more she loved Him. He was truly a great God worthy of worship and praise. He had lifted her up from the deepest pit of sin and made her one of His beloved children. He had taken her—a woman who had grown to hate her own god—and gave her a reason to believe in Him. He had forgiven her of unforgivable sins. He had given her and Lily and Debra and Bilba a second chance, a chance at a life unlike anything they deserved. He had become her God.

Two days later, Salmon was still angry. Who did Rahab the harlot think she was? Infuriating woman! Why did she vex him so?

During the day Salmon railed at Rahab in his thoughts and at Joshua for saddling him with her, but at night he dreamed of her beautiful dark eyes, the curve of her lips, the way she laughed like chimes in the wind. In a dream, he remembered the day he'd smiled at Rahab for the first time.

She'd come out of her tent angry—he had grown to enjoy how she looked when she was, and she seemed to be angry with him a lot. She'd come out of her tent and ran square into his chest.

"Urrr!" she had growled, her head tilted back a little so she could see his face. He'd grabbed her around the waist to keep her from falling, and she had taken it personally.

She'd started beating him in the chest with both fists. "Let me go!"

"Whoa," he'd said. "Slow down there. What did I do now?"

She had glared up at him. "*You* didn't do anything. Not this time."

Then she'd turned and marched back into her tent without saying another word. He'd smiled at her back— not that she would ever find out.

As the days passed, Salmon came to terms with his father's death. With acceptance, some of his anger had melted away. He was ready to start treating Rahab like a human being.

She'd taken his abuse in stride and even praised God for giving him to her as her teacher. Her true character was beginning to show, and that made Salmon feel guilty. God was molding her into someone desirable and beautiful on the inside. She was beginning to pull on his heartstrings. With his anger gone, he could see her as she really was, a beautiful woman who loved God.

Salmon felt someone watching him and snapped out of his reverie. He looked up to see Rahab and Lily and Debra and Bilba approaching him. His heart skipped a beat. Rahab's face looked serene. Her lush lips were inviting. Her shoulders were held high and proud. Her body was perfect, well rounded in all the right spots. Her steps were sure and determined.

"We're ready for our next lesson," she said to him in a voice as soft as the rain.

"Oh. Yes. Of course." Her femininity, her love for God, and her yearning to know more about God was melting his heart.

Salmon was surprised by how quickly Rahab was learning. She actually *wanted* to learn about God. Her willingness to work, her character, and her aptitude for learning drew him to her. He watched in amazement as the Torah brought out and amplified her virtues. Where she was once a diamond in the rough, she now was truly a shining gem.

Rahab caught him staring at her. "What is it?" She wiped her lips, checking for leftover food on her face.

"Nothing," he said with a smile. "I was just…"

Just what? Admiring her beauty? Daydreaming about her? Yes, but he couldn't tell her that. Or could he? Once or twice he'd seen softness in her eyes when she looked his way, but mostly she seemed uncomfortable around him.

The days sped by, quickly turned into weeks, and weeks into months.

"You've changed," Jael said to him one day.

He stopped arranging his pallet and looked at her, eyebrow raised. "How so?"

"The hardness in your eyes has turned into a sparkle. You laugh more," Jael smiled. "She makes you happy, doesn't she?"

"Who?" Salmon pretended he didn't know what she was hinting at.

"You know who, my son. A mother knows when her son has fallen in love."

Fallen in love? He felt an attraction to Rahab, but had he fallen in love with her?

He no longer rushed through lessons to escape from her as quickly as possible. Now he tried to do things for her and Lily. He'd started walking them home after lessons, opening the tent flap for them. Sometimes he stayed around a little while and spent time with them and Dorri. He had long since grown to respect Rahab. But did he love her?

How could I have let this happen? Rahab sighed. She let the robe she was mending fall into her lap and stared at the wall of Dorri's tent.

She knew what men were like. Her life in Jericho had taught her that all men were pigs. What if Salmon was just putting on a façade? What if his change of heart toward her and Lily and her mother and Bilba was just an act? What if, deep down inside, he was no better than Yassib? Rahab shuddered at the thought.

When she'd first entered the camp of Israel, Salmon had despised her and did nothing to hide his feelings, but lately, he had changed. He'd become gentle, and he seemed to enjoy the time they spent together. How could just a few months have made such a difference?

Rahab sighed again, glanced up, and saw her mother giving her a knowing look.

"What?" she asked. "What now?"

"Oh nothing," Debra said, shrugging. "Just thinking."

"Mother, that is not your thinking face. That's your 'I know something you don't' face."

"You wouldn't like it if I told you," her mother said with a teasing smile.

"Try me." Rahab set the robe beside her on her pallet and crossed her arms.

"Just thinking about you and Salmon."

"'Mother," Rahab said firmly, "there is no me and Salmon."

"Oh, but there will be," her mother said with a nod, "there will be."

Could her mother be right? No, no, she couldn't let a man into her life. She knew how men were, but somehow Salmon had broken down her defenses. She had to be careful. She *had* to keep him at a distance. But she felt something for him that she had never felt before for any man.

There was a call from outside the tent. Salmon. Rahab blushed at the thought of his smile.

"Come in," her mother said.

"Salmon!" Lily jumped up from her pallet.

She ran to Salmon and jumped into his arms. Lily really loved him, almost like a daughter loves her father. Salmon knelt down in front of her. Suddenly, he reached out and tickled her. She bent over with giggles.

Bilba stood quietly beside him, her eyes bright and twinkling. She reached forward and grabbed his arm, pulling him off balance. He fell over in a slow, exaggerated way, making Bilba and Lily laugh.

Rahab loved to watch them play. Sometimes they had tickle wars. Sometimes he got down on his hands and knees and gave them rides on his back.

Watching them reminded her of how her father had once been before the near loss of his business had changed him from the father that had loved her unconditionally and cherished her mother into the father that was constantly trying to build his ego by tearing down others. She missed the father she'd had before the monster he became.

Once, when she was about four years old, her family had taken a hike to the Jordan River for the day. Her mother had packed so much food that there was no way they would be able to eat it all. They had played in the river. Her father had stood in the water tossing her high up into the air. She would sail up high and land with a splash. He'd chase her around, tickling her when he caught her.

They had laughed and played while her mother watched from her seat under a palm tree where she was playing with Hagdad, only a year old at the time. Debra had just finished making the blue cotton blanket they were sitting on the week before. She'd smiled and laughed right along with them.

That was her mother before her father had driven her into a deep depression. Would Salmon end up changing like her father had? Would she one day be a shell of what she had once been like her mother had been only months before?

Salmon stopped tickling Lily and rose to his feet, but Lily wasn't ready to give up. She reached up to tickle him in the ribs. He lifted her above his head, tossing her into the air. *He's so strong.* Salmon pulled Lily into an embrace. She threw her arms around his neck and laid her head on his shoulder.

Lily truly did love Salmon. And he truly loved her. Rahab loved that about him. He loved her child.

What would happen if she started to show interest in Salmon and he didn't want it? If he didn't feel the same about her as she felt about him, he'd feel awkward around her. What if he didn't want anything to do with her and Lily anymore? It would crush Lily to lose him.

Salmon turned to Rahab. "Would you like to take a walk with me? The sun will be setting soon, and I know the perfect place to watch it."

She wanted to go, but she said, "I have to put Lily to bed."

"Your mother can do that." His smile lit up the tent, and he winked at Debra. Rahab saw her mother wink back.

What is going on here? Rahab wondered. There was only one way to find out.

"All right," she said and rose to her feet.

They slowly walked side by side toward the outside of the camp, kicking up sand as they went. Rahab noticed that Salmon was dragging his feet like a nervous child. What was he thinking about? He kept looking at her and then looking away as soon as she caught his eye. Was he flirting? When they finally reached her boulder, she sat down beside him, their backs against the rock facing west.

The boulder was warm from the sun's rays beating on it all day long. A lone hawk circled high above. A pair of hedgehogs lay in the sand just a few yards away sunning themselves. A small fly buzzed around Salmon's head, causing him to bat at it incessantly. Rahab smiled and squinted into the western sky. The sun was only moments from being in that stage of setting that blossomed colors all over the dimming sky.

She looked over at Salmon, studying his profile, trying to figure out what was on his mind. "Do you come here often?"

"Yes," Salmon answered. "This is a special place for me. This is where you decided to be part of my life. Well, not my life per se," he looked down, embarrassed, "but part of Israel. Part of my world." He looked up and met her gaze. "I need to apologize."

"For what?" she asked, her voice quavering.

"For the way I treated you at first."

"You already apologized for that."

"I know," he said, "but I didn't feel it when I said it. I *really* am sorry, Rahab."

So that's what this was all about, getting rid of his guilt. If that's what he wanted, she could give it to him.

"It's all right, Salmon." She'd thought he was asking her on a walk because he had feelings for her. Her heart fell. She had hoped…

"It's not all right. It never was." He looked away, his jaw tight. "It never will be."

"Salmon," Rahab said gently, remembering her lessons. "I forgive you."

He turned back to her and smiled. She'd apparently said what he wanted to hear. She was right. He just needed to clear his conscience. No matter how strongly she felt about him, she knew he could never feel the same way about her. Who could love a harlot?

Chapter 17

Rahab reached out and touched the wildflowers growing so lushly beside her. She let her fingers caress the petals, their thick scent drifting up to her. Enveloping her. She listened for the sweet sound of her brother and sisters as they played not far from her. Only she couldn't hear them. She jumped to her feet in a frenzy. She looked around her. No children! Where were they! Her heart beat in her ears. She felt dizzy. She ran in the direction she had last heard them from.

Suddenly, a large Israelite tent reared up in her way. It had popped up out of nowhere. She rushed around it. It seemed to go on forever. Finally, around it, she looked about her. She was in the desert. No beautiful flowers. No rustling grass. Still, no children.

She turned in a full circle. The tent had disappeared. There was nothing. No one. No palm trees. No bunches of grass. No children. Nothing.

She peered up at the hot sun. She could feel it draining the moisture from her. She was thirsty, but there was no water. The sun beat relentlessly on her head and shoulders. She was having a hard time breathing, the heat was so intense. She dropped into the sand. She deserved whatever she got. She had lost the children.

Far away, she saw two figures coming toward her. She stared after them as they came closer. One tall. One small and petite. Salmon? Lily?

She jumped up and ran toward the figures, but the farther she ran, the further they got from her. They slowly disappeared from her sight. She fell to the sand again. Defeated. She started crying in large sobs.

Suddenly, she was sitting in water. It was rapidly rising over her legs, over her navel, over her chest, and over her shoulders. She jumped up, but the water rose with her to her chin. She tried to keep herself afloat by treading water, but it rose to her mouth, and she struggled to keep her head above the water. The current was strong, dragging her under. Over her nose. She pulled against the water with all she had. Over her head. She panicked. She was going to die!

She gave up. Today was her day. There was nothing she could do about it. Suddenly she was on her pallet. She threw back the covers and sat up, coughing and sputtering. She hugged herself. What a dream!

"Mama?" Rahab hadn't noticed that Lily was sitting beside her. Lily picked up her mother's hand and caressed it with the other. "Mama, are you okay?"

Rahab pulled her into a tight embrace and buried her nose in her hair. Sweet Lily.

"Mama?"

"I'm okay, Sweetheart."

"Mama?"

"Yes, Baby?" Rahab sat up and pulled away from Lily just enough to see her face.

"You're squishing me."

Rahab laughed. A light, cheerful laugh. She was truly blessed.

Salmon looked around him. Everything was perfect. He had one of his mother's hand-woven blankets spread on the sand. In the middle was a basket of flatbread, juicy purple grapes, chunks of cheese, and a jar of water. The palm tree beside him cast a perfect shadow over the blanket. The water in the spring beside the tree gurgled out of the ground, making a pleasant backdrop. Soft, fluffy clouds covered the sun. The slight breeze chased the intense heat away but wasn't strong enough to blow sand in the food or to make it chilly. Everything was perfect.

He had worn his best robe. A long, flowing red robe with a belt of white goatskin that had been beaten, pulled, braided and dried into a glossy shine. He had washed his sandals, also made from the soft goatskin, until they shone.

He looked up toward the camp and saw his mother coming with Rahab in tow. She looked clueless. Exactly how he wanted it. She kept stealing glances at his mother and then at him.

"Thank you, Mother," Salmon said with a nod. Jael smiled and then turned to leave.

"What's this all about?" Rahab asked, looking at the blanket and all the food it contained.

"I thought maybe we could get away. Alone. And have some quiet time. Just the two of us."

Rahab looked surprised. She smiled and took a seat on the blanket. Salmon sat down beside her and motioned to the food before them.

"Help yourself," he said.

Rahab reached out and took a grape. She smiled as the juice erupted in her mouth just like it had done in his. He watched her timidly nibble the cheese and bread. He liked to watch her.

"I thought maybe we could get to know each other better. I'll go first. I was born during the time Israel was wandering through the wilderness. I saw a lot of providence from God. He provided manna, small white pieces of bread that tasted like honey. Water is hard to come by in the desert, but we always had enough for all the animals and for all of Israel to have plenty to drink and wash. There were always enough clumps of grass and plains to feed all the animals. Our shoes and clothes grew with us and never wore out. The women had to teach themselves to sew once we reached the Jordan and our clothes stopped growing with us. We had made it to the holy land. Thankfully, some women had been taught by their grandmothers to sew and were able to teach the other women.

"My parents loved me a lot, and I loved them. Then my father died." He looked down at his hands. He swallowed. "I wasn't here to protect him. I was mad at myself. Mad at God. That's why I was so mean to you. Why I was so harsh. I shouldn't have taken it out on you. But I did. And I'm truly sorry." He took another deep breath and looked up at her. He tried to gauge her reaction. Did she believe him? "I guess that's about all. Now, about you."

"You don't really want to know about me." Rahab shrugged and blushed. "My life is a life of sin. I was a harlot. I helped two spies. I met God. I'm here now—today. The end."

Salmon stared deeply into her dark eyes, moist with emotion. She looked down and picked at an imaginary fleck on her robe.

"I want to know everything about you," Salmon said as he reached up to take her hands in his.

Rahab peered into his face. She took a deep breath like she was about to speak, then she let her shoulders slump forward. Salmon waited patiently. He turned her hands over in his and began to rub circles on the back of her hands with his thumbs.

"I ran away from home when I was fourteen," she started, her voice soft and low. "I joined the temple of Astarte as a temple prostitute. I had no choice. It was either that or be forced to marry an awful, hateful brute named Yassib. Father needed the dowry money to keep his fish business afloat. Father didn't care that Yassib would beat me and even try to kill me if I married him. He didn't care about me. Didn't care enough to protect me. So, I had to protect myself, and becoming a temple prostitute was the only way out.

"I didn't intend to become a temple prostitute the day I went to the temple. It just sort of happened. When every young woman reaches marrying age, she has to sit in the temple courtyard and wait for a man to choose her to have relations. Only after she's chosen can she marry. I was praying so hard that no one would choose me so I wouldn't have to marry Yassib. But I was chosen very quickly by Yassib himself. He raped me. Took my virginity. He publicly forced himself upon me, and I couldn't do anything about it. Yassib came to the temple at least once a week after that to abuse my services and to abuse me.

"Knowing we'd have to sacrifice our firstborn should we get pregnant, the girls and I started taking herbs to keep from getting pregnant. But it was too late for one of us." Rahab looked down at her hands and carefully drew them out of Salmon's grasp like she had just noticed he was caressing them. She crossed her arms in front of her in a protective gesture.

165

"My best friend, Star, was already pregnant. Star became odder and odder during the pregnancy. After she gave birth, she lost her mind completely. She ended up killing herself." Rahab took a deep breath as a lone tear streaked down her cheek. She brushed the tear away with the back of her hand. "She made me promise to care for Lily."

"Lily is not yours?" Salmon asked in disbelief. He'd just always assumed. "You're so good with her. I thought she was yours."

"She is. Now."

Salmon waited for Rahab to continue. He stared into her face. She was so brave. She'd been through so much, yet she was solid. Unbroken. Amazing.

"If it hadn't been for Lily, I don't know what I would've done," Rahab continued. "I would've lost my mind. Or taken my life like Star did. To escape Yassib.

"After my contract was up with the temple, Lily and I bought the house on the wall where I hid you and Andrew. We tried to turn it into an inn and restaurant, but no one came. No one would do business with a woman who'd been a temple prostitute. I was forced to return to harlotry to support my little family.

"It was a very prosperous business. I grew to hate the men who came to use me more and more. Yassib even more. I looked for a way out, but I couldn't find one. Then you and Andrew came. Israel took Jericho, and I was free. Free from harlotry. Free from the pigs that abused my services. Free from Yassib. And, yes, I gloried in his death." Rahab looked behind her shoulder like she expected to see someone standing there. "I know now that it was wrong, but I was happy to see him dead that day. My torments were over."

Rahab peered back up into Salmon's eyes and forced a tiny smile. They took their time eating, reveling in each other's company, but soon their food was gone, and it was getting on to late afternoon.

Rahab stood. "This has been nice, but I really need to get back to Lily."

Salmon stood with her, then reached down to gather the leftover food and the pitcher. "I'll see you tomorrow for our lesson, then?"

Rahab nodded curtly, turned, and walked away.

Salmon watched her go. She hadn't said how she felt about the outing other than "it was nice." Had she enjoyed his company as much as he'd enjoyed hers? Would she ever be open to a "them?"

With each passing day, Salmon felt himself fall more and more in love with Rahab. But he was torn. She had been a harlot. Could he trust her to stay faithful to him? Could she trust herself?

"Dearest God, The great I AM, I don't know what to do. Please, help me." He let out a sigh. He didn't feel any better. Was God listening? He knew some answers didn't come right away. He'd just have to trust God. "If this is not meant to be, please take my love for this woman out of my heart."

Salmon didn't know how Rahab felt about him. What if he just made a fool of himself by expressing his love for her? What if… No. It didn't matter. He couldn't allow himself to follow that train of thought. How he felt didn't matter if God didn't condone it. He wanted to pursue Rahab, but was a relationship with her against God? She was a Canaanite, and God had expressly forbidden Israel to marry the heathen of the land. But Rahab wasn't a heathen. She had quickly adapted to Israel's way of life. She had become, in every area of her life, an Israelite. He'd have to talk to his great uncle. Joshua would know the answer.

Chapter 18

Salmon ran into Joshua a few days later. His heart jumped. Did he really want to ask his great uncle such a personal question? Did he really want Joshua to know about his feelings for Rahab? He needed to know if his feelings for her were forbidden, but at the same time, he didn't want to know. What if Joshua said the relationship couldn't be? That answer would crush his heart. Could he endure yet another blow? Maybe not, but Rahab was worth it.

Salmon rushed to catch up with him. "Uncle."

Joshua turned to face him. He stood there looking at Salmon as he tried to make the words come from his mouth. He wrinkled his brow in concentration.

"I have a problem," he finally said, his breathing rapid due to the anxiety rising in his chest.

Joshua relaxed a little. He didn't look like he was standing at attention anymore. He nodded his head. "Go on."

Salmon looked down at his trembling hands, calloused from the rough work he did every day, swallowed hard, and took a deep breath. He smelled cooking fires, wet goatskins, and musty dirt. He longed for Rahab's smell. He'd never been around anyone who always smelled like wildflowers. How did she do it?

"I sort of fell in love with someone perhaps I should not have," Salmon said, kicking at the dirt, "and I don't know what to do."

"Rahab?" Joshua's tense face turned up in a smile, the smile even reaching his eyes.

Salmon's mouth fell open. "How did you know?" He had tried so hard to hide it. At least he thought he did.

"Anyone with two eyes can see that." Joshua smiled wider.

If he's not careful, his face will crack, Salmon thought.

"Is it that obvious?" A smile began to form on Salmon's face.

"You follow her around like a newly born calf does his mother." Joshua laughed, then he stared long and hard at Salmon.

Salmon could feel beads of sweat forming on his brow. The heat was not the cause of the sweat; the cause was from the questions he still had to ask.

"So, what is your problem?" Joshua prodded.

"Is it against God's Law? I mean, to love Rahab. Is it okay?" The words tumbled out. Salmon wasn't sure if Joshua would be able to untangle them enough for the question to make sense.

Joshua draped his arm across Salmon's shoulders and prompted him to walk forward with him. "When Rahab chose to become an Israelite, God accepted her as one of His own. God grafted her in, making her an Israelite. You are free to court Rahab. If you were not, I would have told you when I first noticed your feelings for her."

Joshua stopped and turned toward Salmon. "You have my blessing, nephew." Joshua patted his shoulder and turned away.

"Thank you," Salmon said, feeling tears well up in his eyes, but Joshua was already too far away to hear.

He had never been one to cry, but he had cried a lot, almost nonstop, since his father died. No, that wasn't entirely true. He'd been crying less since Rahab started making her way into his heart. Part of him had healed, and he hadn't even noticed.

Salmon fought back the tears of joy and went to find Rahab. Now that he knew God condoned his relationship, he had to tell Rahab. Would she accept him? A battle warred within his mind. What if she didn't want him?

Rahab lifted the heavy water jug up onto her shoulder. She had built muscle since she'd come to live among the Israelites. The many chores were physically demanding. In Jericho, the only thing she'd had to do was care for Lily and please her male customers. She'd had servants to do the rest. When she'd first come to Israel's camp only five short months ago, she could barely lift an empty clay jug. They were large, reaching a little less than knee high and were quite heavy, but now she could lift it, full of water, high enough for it to rest upon her shoulder.

As she walked back toward Dorri's tent, she saw Salmon coming toward her, a radiant smile upon his face. Her heart leaped within her. His smile always made her heart flutter. He smiled often, but this smile was different. Wider. Bigger. What was he up to?

"Rahab, I need to talk with you."

"Let me put this water inside the tent." She turned and set the jug down. She'd put it where it went later.

Salmon took one of her hands in his, rubbing circles on the back of it with his thumb. "Rahab." She liked it when he said her name. "I need to tell you something. To ask you something."

Rahab smiled. Why did he look so nervous?

With his free hand, Salmon reached up and touched the end of one of her braids, rolling it between his fingers. Then he ran his finger along her jawline, tracing it from her ear to her chin. She leaned into his touch. He was always so gentle. He turned his hand, placing his balled fist beneath her chin and used his thumb to caress her lips. Was he going to kiss her? Would she let him?

He dropped his hand to his side, then reached out and gently took her hand in his. Rahab felt disappointed. She was surprised at her reaction. She really *had* wanted him to kiss her!

"Uh." He paused.

She lifted her eyebrows, urging him to go on. He looked down at her hands. He smiled. She loved his smile. He looked back up into her face.

He cleared his throat. Taking much too long. "How has your day been?"

She again raised her eyebrows. She knew that wasn't his question. Why was he stalling? She didn't answer.

He took a deep breath, letting his chest swell big as he breathed in, letting out his breath slowly. Much too slowly.

"I want to marry you. To make you my wife. I love you. I have for a while." Salmon talked fast. "Will you be my wife?" His face turned red. He bit his lip and looked down at their hands once more, awaiting her response.

Rahab didn't know what to say. Yesterday she'd been confused, wondering what had sparked the idea of a picnic in Salmon's mind. She hadn't been sure if he was even interested in her, and today he was proposing marriage? She slowly withdrew her hand. Did she love him? She searched her heart.

"No." She watched his face fall, his heart crushed. "Not yet."

Salmon looked into her eyes, a half smile on his lips. "So it's not a no? Just a not yet?"

Rahab smiled weakly. "Not yet."

He reached out and took her hand again, playing with the ends of her fingers. His eyes searched hers. His beautiful blue eyes.

Rahab didn't know what she felt for him. Maybe it *was* love, but could she admit it? How could she ever love a man after experiencing how rough and cruel they could be? But Salmon was different. She'd never seen him even look at another woman with lust. Maybe she could love him. She just wasn't sure yet.

Now it was Rahab's turn to draw a deep breath. "I just need some time."

Salmon sat in his tent a few hours later doing nothing. Staring off into space. When Rahab had said no, his world had fallen apart. How could she say no? Had he misread her signals? Did she feel nothing for him? No, she must—she'd said, "Not yet." The words gave him hope. He breathed a sigh of relief. It wasn't a no!

His heart soared. "Not yet." That meant, "Yes. Someday." He could wait.

Suddenly, the shofar sounded long and loud. Joshua was calling for an assembly. Salmon hurried toward the tabernacle, where the meetings were always held. He tripped on his feet, still elated that Rahab was considering his proposal. Catching himself, he looked around to see if anyone had noticed. No one seemed to see or care.

When the people were gathered, Joshua climbed up on a rock so they could all see him. Their murmuring stopped when he raised his hands for silence.

"Tomorrow, we march on Ai. God has instructed us to conquer the land of Canaan," Joshua said, his voice strong and loud, "and Ai is the most plausible choice."

His announcement was met with cheers.

"Joshua!" Someone called out near the front of the congregation. His voice was low and gravelly but boomed loud enough to be heard by many of the congregation.

Joshua looked at the man. His face showed confusion then turned up in a smile. He gestured toward the man, motioning for him to speak.

"Let not all the people go. Let about two or three thousand men go up and smite Ai. It is but a small city."

"This is true." Joshua nodded his head. "Ai is small. Three thousand men will go up against the city. All the rest will stay here. I will announce who will go this evening. Be ready to be called upon again."

Joshua lowered his hand, dispersing the congregation.

Salmon spent the rest of the day cleaning his mother's tent. He had long since moved back in with her. His periodic visits after his father's death hadn't been enough to help her through her grief. She needed someone to look after her. To make sure she ate and slept.

Salmon needed something to keep his mind busy while Israel awaited the evening assembly. He couldn't bear to dwell on the possibility of being chosen to fight in another battle. Though they were fewer and farther in between, he was still having horrible nightmares centering on the battle of Jericho and the deaths he had caused.

He slowly took the tent apart. He had seen his mother do it many times, but it was harder than it looked. He kept getting tangled up in the mess he was creating. Finally finished, flustered, he carried the skins to the Jordan River, two at a time, and washed them, scrubbing the goat hair with wet sand. The periodic rainfall made the skins smell musty. The scent wafted up to him as he scrubbed. The smell had been bothering him for weeks. It was time to scrub it away.

Reconstructing the tent was harder than it seemed. He couldn't figure out which hide went where so all the sides would be covered. When he finished, he had a lopsided mess.

"I'm sorry, Mother," he said sheepishly, his cheeks blushed red as he stared down at his work-worn hands. He had failed again.

"Don't worry about it, my son." Jael smiled, patted him on the back and chuckled. "Your old mother is used to cleaning up your messes."

Over the next hour, Jael directed him on which hides to place where. Salmon followed her instructions, and soon, the tent was put back together.

"That is much better," Jael said with a smile.

Salmon took a deep breath. Yes, and it smelled much better too.

He looked up as Rahab and Lily walked around the side of the tent hand in hand. "You look like you've been working hard," she said with a smile.

She smiled at him. Dare he hope?

"It needed to be done," he smiled back at her. He couldn't keep from smiling when she was around.

Lily ran to Salmon. He swung her up into the air. He would never get used to her squeals of delight. They did his heart good. If Rahab became his wife, Lily would become his daughter. His heart warmed. He couldn't wait.

"We're having roasted quail and flatbread for dinner tonight," Rahab said, looking from Salmon to Jael. "Lily would like you to join us."

Lily placed one of her small hands on each side of his face and turned his head to face her. "Please?" she asked.

How could he refuse her? "Of course."

"Yay!" She pushed away from Salmon and slid down to the ground. "Are you coming too?" She asked his mother, her eyes sparkling.

"Why not?" Jael smiled down at Lily. "Roasted quail sounds good."

That evening, Israel came together again for the announcement. Salmon's stomach was in knots. He was glad dinner would be after the assembly. He prayed his name wouldn't be called.

Joshua called out the families that would go up to battle. That was easier than calling out individuals.

Salmon listened as many families were called. Surely Joshua was nearing the end.

"Of the tribe of Judah, the family of Ram."

Salmon's heart sank. The world stood still. He felt like he couldn't breathe. Like something was choking him. He was of the family of Ram. That meant he had to go into battle once again.

Chapter 19

"We leave at first light," Joshua had told the group of those chosen to fight at Ai.

His uncle's words hung over Salmon like a dark cloud. He felt like running into the desert to hide, but he forced himself to walk toward his tent where he saw Rahab standing and waiting for him. They had gotten separated in the crowd during the cheering and confusion that ensued after Joshua had chosen those who were to march on Ai.

He couldn't let anyone know how he felt. Everyone else seemed pleased to be chosen. After all, they were marching toward victory. Surely after taking Jericho, Ai would fall quickly. God was with them.

Salmon took Rahab in his arms, and she crumbled into him.

"Why?" She whispered into his chest.

"I don't know," he replied, his breath teasing loose strands of her hair. He tried to hold back the tears that were pressing on his eyelids.

"Oh, Salmon!" his mother, Jael, wailed as she stumbled toward him.

Her eyes were puffy and red. Tears ran down her cheeks. Salmon let go of Rahab and opened his arms toward his mother, but she stopped short of his embrace.

"How could he?" Jael said between sobs. "I'll talk to Joshua! He will make it right. Surely, he'll not make you go. My husband is dead, and you are my only son!"

Salmon stepped closer to Jael, but she stepped back from him and crossed her arms protectively. He sighed, taking a deep breath so he wouldn't start crying too.

"Mother, we must accept Joshua's decision."

"Maybe Joshua doesn't know he chose you," Jael rambled on as if Salmon had never spoken. "Maybe it was an accident."

"No, mother," Salmon said. "I have to go, and that is that."

"But Joshua can fix it!" she said as sobs began again.

Salmon reached out and rubbed his mother's shoulder and upper arm. He bent down so he could look her in the eyes. "It's okay to cry, but we must accept God's decision."

Finally, Jael allowed herself to be pulled into Salmon's embrace.

"I know," she whispered. "I'm just so scared of losing you."

"I know mother." *I'm scared too.*

Rahab reached from behind him and rubbed circles on his upper back. Salmon half-turned to face her and pulled her into an awkward embrace, Jael in one arm and Rahab in the other. He lowered his head and smelled Rahab's hair. If only she'd agree to marry him, he'd be the happiest man in the world, war or not.

The next morning Salmon stepped outside to breathe in the day. It had dawned bright and cheerful, full of awe-inspiring color that spread itself over the distant clouds, the extreme opposite of how Salmon felt. His stomach was in knots. Fog filled his brain. He couldn't think. His head hung low; his shoulders slumped. He took a deep breath, trying to cleanse his lungs. It didn't work. He still felt the weight of the world settled upon him.

He didn't have far to go to reach his own tent. He had left all his things in his own tent when he moved to his mother's. It was easier to walk over to his own tent when he needed things than it was to transfer everything over.

Stepping inside, the stale air assaulted him. It had been a while since he had opened the tent up to air it out. He stood still and looked around. Maybe one day this tent would belong to him *and* Rahab. Maybe… if he wasn't killed in battle.

He strapped his armor on. His breastplate, leg guards, and helmet felt much heavier than normal. He pulled up his robe from the back and up between his legs. He wrapped it securely in his belt in preparation for battle. As he smoothed down his cotton britches, where arranging his robe had hiked them up, he realized how slowly he was moving. He'd have to speed up if he was going to meet the rest of the army in time.

He quickly strapped his long sword at his side. His father had given him the intricately designed sword. He loved the scroll shaped handle and the ruby inlay, but he'd always thought it was much too beautiful for war. He didn't want to use it, but it was all he had.

His helmet, once his father's, was a little big but it fit well enough. He suddenly felt even grimmer. The sword, the helmet, they had been his father's. He was suddenly more aware of the hole the death of his father had left in his life.

He picked up his shield, sliding his arm through the larger arm hold and grasping the handle. *Time to go.* He pushed the flap on his tent back and stepped out into the dawning light. He took another deep breath, trying to calm himself.

Rahab stepped from behind the neighboring tent. She stood, hands clasped in front of her, and stared at him, a look of dread upon her face.

"I'm so scared," she finally said, a whimper in her voice.

Tears sprang in Salmon's eyes. He could feel himself beginning to fall apart. He was scared, too.

"I… I don't want to lose you."

Rahab reached out and touched his arm.

This was more emotion than Salmon could handle right now. If he stood here looking at her any longer, the woman he loved, he'd fall apart. He launched himself forward, pushing his way past her.

"Salmon," she said in almost a whisper behind him.

"Salmon, I love you, and I want to marry you. Please be careful out there."

"I love you, Rahab." Salmon only half-turned toward her to hide the tears coursing down his cheeks. "We'll talk when I get back."

Once again, he dragged forward, wanting to look back at the woman he loved, but not daring to. Rahab, the woman he was going to marry. If he came back alive.

Rahab wanted to wail but didn't. She clasped her hands together and sucked a deep breath, trying to be as brave as Salmon. She had left Lily with her mother so she could talk to Salmon before he left. She had accepted his proposal, so he wouldn't go off to war doubting her intentions.

Now if she could keep herself together, keep from running after him. She took a deep breath, trying to calm herself, and decided to go for a walk. She couldn't face Lily's questions right now.

She wandered around the camp, going nowhere in particular. She kept peering toward the eastern sky. It looked like there was a storm moving in. An hour ago, the dark clouds had been barely noticcablc. Now they were building and darkening the sky. *God, be with Salmon. Please keep him safe.*

Hearing a noise in the distance, she looked to the north. She saw the army, with Salmon somewhere in its midst marching away. Tears sprung into her eyes again. Would God allow him to return safely?

Salmon saw Ai ahead. The men of Ai were ready for them. They were all in their armor and lined up in front of Ai five deep in a line that stretched almost the length of the city wall. The city was much smaller than Jericho; still, the gathering of soldiers looked menacing.

The captain, Garghan, called the army of Israel to a halt. "We can do this, men! God goes with us!"

181

He turned and started the army marching toward Ai once more. As they drew near Ai, the city's army started to move toward Israel.

"Attack!" Garghan shouted, waving his sword toward the oncoming army as the Levites blew their trumpets, spreading the command to those who hadn't heard.

Israel broke into a run toward Ai. The two armies clashed all too soon for Salmon, swords clanging against swords and shields. Soldiers grunted. Sweat poured. Both armies fought with all they had, thrusting and jabbing.

Suddenly, Ai started to push Israel back. Israel was defeated!

"Retreat!" Garghan shouted out. The trumpets sounded the alarm of retreat.

Israel turned and ran with Ai on their heels. Salmon began to wheeze as he ran, shocked and stunned by the retreat. His muscles hurt, screaming for oxygen. He could barely run and began to fall back, closer to the army of Ai, closer to impending death. Everyone was passing him. He could feel the soldiers of Ai bearing down upon him.

Salmon felt a stab of cold steel in his back. He stumbled and fell forward, catching himself with his hands. He felt a deep chill shoot through him. He had been stabbed just below his shoulder. He'd had a feeling of dread since he'd found out he was going into battle. He'd known from the beginning that today was his day to die.

Rahab was keenly aware of the rain as it began to pelt down on the tent. From inside, it sounded like little drums tapping the death march. She tried to busy herself around the tent. *Salmon will be fine. He has to be.*

She was trying to mend Bilba and Lily's clothes. They were both growing so fast that Rahab could barely keep their robes long enough.

"Momma? Are you okay?" Lily stood beside her, caressing her arm, rubbing little circles on her elbow.

Rahab started. She'd been sitting with the mending in her lap, doing nothing. She was hundreds of miles away. Not hundreds, but as far as it was from Israel's camp to the city of Ai.

"Momma's okay, sweetheart. I'm just thinking."

"Salmon will be okay, Momma." Lily always seemed to know what she was thinking. "God told me so."

Lily looked up at Rahab with her big brown eyes. Her full cheeks plumped as a smile overtook her face. Both of her dimples deepened as they always did when her smile was genuine. She picked up Rahab's hand and held it gently in hers.

Rahab sighed. Oh to have the faith of a child. "Sweetheart, God doesn't tell us things in that way. He speaks to us through His prophets."

She didn't want to take away Lily's belief that everything would be okay, but she didn't want her to think God had let them down if Salmon didn't come home. *Don't think like that!*

"Well, He told me," Lily insisted. Bilba stood beside her, a faint smile flickering across her face.

Rahab set her stitching on the hides covering the floor of the tent and reached for Lily, pulling her up into her lap. She cuddled her against her chest—their favorite way to cuddle—and began stroking her hair. She wasn't going to argue with her child. Let her believe what she wanted. Maybe it would help her not be so fretful. Rahab wished she could believe that God would bring him home safe.

"Everything okay here?" Rahab's mother asked, knowing exactly what was going on.

Rahab looked at her and nodded hesitantly. Everything *would* be okay. She just had to believe it.

"Here they come!" Someone shouted in an excited voice.

Rahab jumped to her feet, almost knocking Lily to the floor, and rushed out of the tent.

A runner had reached the camp before the army did.

"We lost thirty-six men," he announced breathlessly.

A murmur of worry went through those who were waiting. Everyone wondered if their loved one was part of the thirty-six. Rahab's heart sank. *Let him be okay. Please!*

She pushed her way to the front of the crowd. The soldiers looked dejected. Their heads hung. Their shoulders slumped. Rahab looked for Salmon. There were joyful reunions between soldiers and their families—but Salmon didn't come.

Rahab heard Salmon's mother wail beside her. Rahab turned and pulled her into a close embrace. She sobbed into Rahab's shoulder.

"Please, God. Not my son, too," she whispered. "Not my son, too."

Please, God, no! Hot tears ran down Rahab's face. She raised her head, her eyes searching the distant horizon. Maybe he had stayed behind for some reason, maybe to help carry home the dead. Maybe... But no one was there. No lone figure on the horizon. No Salmon.

Chapter 20

Rahab trudged slowly back toward her tent. Salmon's mother, Jael, clung to her left arm, using Rahab to steady and to lead her. Dorri held Jael from the other side, her arm around her waist. Rahab was in a daze. She couldn't believe this was happening. Had Salmon offended God? Had Jael? Surely there had to be a reason. Maybe Rahab was being punished for something *she* had done.

Lily was holding onto Rahab's skirts from behind. She knew something was happening, something bad. Her mother and Miss Jael were crying, but she didn't know why.

They pushed their way through the throngs of people whose families were complete. Rahab heard excited whispers. People were hugging, clinging to one another. Men were relaying what had happened step by step. Women were giggling and lifting their voices in praise to God. Children snuggled comfortably in their mothers' and fathers' arms wondering why they were receiving so much extra attention, but not minding it a bit. Those too big to be carried were traipsing along behind, smiling up at their parents. People were happy, and they had reason to be. Rahab's spirits dropped lower.

They soon reached the tent and stepped inside. Dorri had dinner on, lamb chops, cactus hearts, and fry-bread. Rahab didn't feel like eating. Her stomach was in knots. She could taste bile in her throat.

Debra looked up as they entered. Her smile quickly faded, her forehead creasing in worry.

"Rahab? What's wrong?"

Rahab couldn't hold her tears any longer. They spilled over onto her cheeks in torrents. Debra rushed to her and pulled her into an embrace. When Rahab was able to get her sobs under control. She pulled away from her mother and looked into her eyes.

"It's Salmon. He didn't return with the others. They said there are many dead, and Salmon didn't return. Oh, Mother!"

She fell into her mother's embrace once more and let her hold her like she used to when she was a child.

When they finally pulled apart, Lily let go of her mother and skipped after her meemaw. Lily crawled into Debra's lap as she lowered herself onto her pallet. Lily put her arms around her neck and stretched up to place a light kiss on her cheek. She then nestled her head in her meemaw's chest, soft and comforting.

Rahab saw a flicker of regret appear on Debra's face, a longing, she knew, for Aliyan, but it passed as quickly as it had appeared. Debra laid her cheek on the top of her granddaughter's head.

Rahab smiled. Lily could always make Debra smile despite any circumstance. Rahab returned her attention to Jael, pulling her closer, once again wrapping her arms around her. She was still shuddering, but her sobbing had slowed. Rahab looked down at the top of her head. Jael's black hair, sprinkled with gray, was curly, unusually mussed and unruly. Jael's hair was always neat and tidy, but not today. And who could blame her?

Her frail body melted into Rahab's. Much thinner than Rahab, Jael's petite frame made her appear small and fragile. But she was far from fragile. Emotionally, she was the strongest person Rahab had ever met. Her physical strength was nothing to be tousled with either. Rahab wouldn't want to get into a fight with her.

Rahab was standing, supporting Jael's weight as well as her own. Her back and shoulder muscles were screaming for release, but she wouldn't move. Not until Jael was ready. Finally, Jael pulled away and wiped the tears from her face. Rahab wasn't sure if she was all cried out or if she had one again tapped into that inner strength.

Rahab listened to the joyous sounds going on outside the tent. Many people were congregating in the area around their tent trying to find out what had happened and if their family was home safely. She could hear quiet laughing. Happiness. How could they be so jubilant when there were families torn apart by the wretchedness of war? How could they be so happy when the war had been lost? At the same time, Rahab knew that if Salmon had returned, she'd be among them, rejoicing in the fact that her man was safely home.

A woman stepped into the tent; medium build, medium height, nothing spectacular about her. Olive skin, long kinky curly hair, and big blue eyes. Maybe in her mid-thirties. She stood there looking from face to face. Rahab, Jael, Debra, and even Lily stared at her expectantly.

"We're having games," she said, her hand pressed to her slightly rounded belly. She was, Rahab thought, maybe twenty weeks along with child. "We're gathering to play knuckles while we wait for the rescue party to return with news of our husbands and sons."

"Did you say rescue party?" Rahab asked, taking a step toward her.

The woman nodded. "They just left. There may be some survivors. Until they return, we need something to keep our minds occupied. Until we know for sure." She paused and looked at each of them in turn again. "Would you care to join us?"

A rescue party! Rahab clasped her hands in front of her and said a prayer of thanks to God. She hadn't thought of this, that Salmon may have survived, that he might be laying out there waiting for rescue. Her energy was renewed. All of a sudden, she felt antsy. She couldn't wait until the rescue party returned. Surely Salmon would be found, and surely, he would be alright. He would be home soon.

Yes, she decided. Yes. Games to keep her mind busy while she waited would be good.

"Okay." Rahab nodded her head. "I'm coming." She looked at Jael, who shook her head. She wasn't interested. But she'd be okay here with Dorri and Debra to keep her company.

The walk to the woman's tent was slow and long. Trekking around the tight crowds of clingy people added to the trip.

"Here we are," the woman said. "By the way, I'm Mary." She held out her hand.

"Rahab," she said, grasping the offered hand.

They stepped inside the tent, too warm from the fire burning in the center. Seven women looked up from where they were sitting on goatskins scattered on the floor. Women of all ages, women waiting to hear if their husbands, sons, or grandsons were going to make it home. It was a somber group. Their faces looked grim. Their brows were furrowed and their minds a million miles away.

Rahab managed a small smile in response to the women's curious glances. She knew this was the first time many of them had seen her. With dark skin, darkened even more by the sun and hair braided tightly to her head, she looked different. Differences drew curiosity and sometimes contempt. She looked around to see if any of the women disapproved of her being a part of their group and only saw saddened faces and blank stares. She was free to join.

"Have you ever played Knuckles before?" Mary asked.

Rahab shook her head.

"We use these." Mary held five small bones in her hand, dried, clean, and white. "They're actually the pastern bone of the goats and sheep we slaughter. You can see they look different on each side."

Rahab picked up one of the bones and studied it. It had two rounded ends, two narrow sides, one concave and one convex, and two broad sides, again one concave and one convex. She ran her fingers over the bone, feeling only smoothness.

"We throw them up in the air and how they land tells us how many points a person gets." Mary pointed to the different sides of the bone Rahab was holding as she explained. "The convex broad side is counted as three points. The convex narrow side, the chios, is one point. If the concave narrow side lands up, you get six points, and the concave broad side is counted as four points. You can make up to a total of thirty points in one throw." Mary gently took the bone Rahab was still holding in her hand. "Do you understand?"

"Yes."

"Good," Mary smiled. "You go first."

They played long into the night. Rahab often wondered if the rescue party was having any success. They were still gone. Surely that had to be a good sign. The women all talked during the game. Rahab got to know each of them by name.

189

Deborah, similar to her mother's name, was short and thin. Her black hair was waist length and curly. Her blue eyes were always smiling, even though she was not. She was hopeful in awaiting the return of her husband—middle-aged, stocky, and tall. The best-looking man in Israel according to her testimony.

Elizabeth sat the whole time, so Rahab wasn't sure of her stature. She sat slumped, shoulders hung low, head jutted forward, elbows on her crisscrossed knees. She was waiting to hear news about her grandson, Deborah's husband.

In the far corner of the tent, not playing the game, but there simply because she didn't want to be alone while she awaited news of her son, was Eden. She was quiet, maybe just because of her worry, her fear that her baby, her only son, was dead. Her husband was home, sleeping, she presumed. It wasn't that he didn't care, she had told them in a solemn voice; it was that he had been ill and needed his rest to heal.

The last player was Leah. She was the youngest person there, seventeen years old, and she was waiting to hear of her husband. They had married a little over a year ago and had fallen in love very quickly. Her father had chosen a great match for her. They fit together like a pair of handcrafted shoes. Rahab could tell through her eyes when she talked of Abraham that she truly did love him. *Please, God let Leah's husband be all right. She needs him as I need Salmon. Let Salmon be okay.*

"Thank you, ladies," Rahab said with a smile. "I have enjoyed spending time with you, but I should really get back and see how Jael is doing."

The women all nodded their heads in agreement and sent a small smile her way.

Rahab trudged back toward Dorri's tent, hoping she could find her way back. All of the crowds had dispersed long ago. She had listened during their game

190

as the crowds thinned and the noise dissipated. Now she walked through the camp, alone in the world.

She took a deep breath. The air felt heavy and moist. She tilted her head back to see the stars, bright and cheerful, twinkling, singing the praises of God. The full moon caught her attention. It wasn't long ago that she thought of the full moon as a good omen from Astarte. Now she knew the truth; she knew the Creator.

Would the rescue party return with Salmon? If he were injured, would he recover? If she lost Salmon, she didn't know what she would do. She reveled in the love she felt for him and hoped that love would be enough to pull her through.

Chapter 21

Salmon groaned as he tried to roll onto his back. He felt weak and shaky. The army of Ai had retreated into the city hours ago. They had left him for dead, but he was alive! How had he escaped when so many had died? How many children would be fatherless? How many wives husbandless? How many parents bereft of a son?

"Hello!" Someone shouted, their voice thick with emotion, slurring their Hebrew a bit.

"Hello!" Another voice came, quieter, further away.

A rescue party!

"I'm here!" Salmon tried to yell, but his voice sounded faint in his ears. "Over here!"

His vision was blurred, but he thought he saw someone moving toward him. Then he slipped out of consciousness again.

When next he came to, he felt himself being moved. He blinked his eyes open and saw two men were carrying him on a gurney. The Israelites used a gurney to transport the sick when they moved camp. They were made of two long poles with cloth stretched between them that made sort of a hammock. They were carried, one man in the front and one man in the back. The side-to-side swaying of the gurney made him feel queasy, and, bless it all, it hurt!

The rising sun was hidden behind clouds. The sky was dark and dreary. The rain fell softly, landing with a little plop and running down his face. The sky was usually full of birds, but no birds flew about today. Maybe it was just his injuries, but the day seemed surreal.

The camp came into view. No one stood there awaiting his return. They must have gone home hours ago. Did they think him dead? He felt for his mother. After losing her husband not so long ago, it would be tragic to lose her son, too.

How was Rahab? Was she broken too? She'd told him she wanted to marry him—that she loved him, but had she said that simply because emotions were running high? Did she truly mean what she'd said? Would she be mourning him as well?

He was carried into his mother's tent. He was acutely aware of the smell of musty skins. Again. And he had just washed the tent! The air inside seemed dry and full of static. Why were his senses so heightened?

"Salmon!" He heard a screech. "Oh, Salmon!" His mother rushed to his side and buried her face in the chest of his dirty robe and began to cry, her shoulders shaking.

Salmon stifled a moan, his face contorting. He wanted to allow his mother to revel in her rejoicing, but her embrace caused him so much pain.

Finally, his mother stood up and moved aside. Rahab stood there staring at him, tears in her eyes. "Salmon."

That was all she needed to say. Her voice was full of love. He knew then that she was his. Now and forever.

The doctor came in moments after he had been laid on his pallet. He used to be tall but now stooped, bent over with age. His white hair, longer than most Israelites, was soaked with rain but still had volume due to his rolling curls. His hands looked large and capable.

He rolled Salmon up onto his side. "You have wet sand packed in your wound. That's good because it stopped the bleeding." The doctor's tender hands softly caressed the wound. "Now it's bad because I have to clean it all out of there before I can stitch you up."

Salmon groaned. This was going to hurt.

Rahab waited outside the tent with Lily and Bilba while the doctor cleaned out and stitched Salmon's wound.

She reminisced while she waited. She'd been lying awake on her pallet in Dorri's tent when she heard voices outside. She'd rushed outside to see the rescue parties returning, some of the searchers carrying gurneys between them.

"Salmon? Do any of you have Salmon?" She had rushed from gurney to gurney, checking each one carefully.

In the end, there had been no Salmon. She'd rushed to his mother's tent. Hoping. Two of the searchers were just leaving the tent. She'd rushed inside to see Salmon's mother bent over a gurney, pulling her son into an embrace.

Thank You, God, for bringing him home to me.

The birds were starting to tweet again as they always did after a rain. One lone bird flew from tent top to tent top like it was trying to find the most comfortable perch. She looked off to the east to see a beautiful big rainbow. She'd learned in her lessons that the first rainbow God ever made was as a promise to Noah to never flood the whole earth again. She loved rainbows—the colors so bright. The bow of promise.

"Mama?" Lily tugged on Rahab's sleeve. "Is Salmon going to be okay?" Her grave face looked up into hers. She looked beaten down, devastated. Bilba stood beside her, face pale and hands nervously entwined.

Rahab wished she could wipe all their worries away, but Rahab didn't know the answer. She knelt down, took both of Lilly's hands in hers before reaching out with one hand and grasping one of Bilba's.

"Let's ask God to help him." She bowed her head. "Dear God, you know how much we love Salmon. Please help him get well soon. Amen."

"Amen," Lily repeated in her soft angelic voice.

Lily and Bilba's faces brightened a bit.

Rahab thought over her prayer. Everything she'd said was true. She *did* truly love Salmon. She'd had doubts after telling Salmon before he went to war. She knew she'd been an emotional wreck. She shouldn't have told him that. She should have waited until she'd known for sure. This time, in her prayer, she'd admitted the truth to God, the God who loved her and knew her heart long before she did.

She'd already decided to marry Salmon, not long after he had asked, but purely out of convenience. She needed someone to take care of her and Lily. She hadn't been sure whether she loved him or not. She was sure she would grow to love him over time. Now, she realized, she truly did love him. She would tell him soon, but now wasn't the time.

The doctor walked solemnly out the tent. Rahab looked at him expectantly. He nodded to her and walked on to see his next patient. Why hadn't he told her anything about Salmon? She, Bilba, and Lily trudged into the tent. Salmon's mother sat on the ground next to his pallet, holding his hand in hers.

She turned when she heard them come in. "He's going to be just fine." She smiled endearingly. "God has brought him through. The doctor said he just needs rest. His wound should heal up quickly. He'll be back a few times in the next few days to make sure no infection sets in."

Rahab sank to the ground next to her and reached out to pull her into a hug. Salmon was going to be all right!

That evening Joshua called another meeting. Once the people were gathered, he spoke. "There has been a trespass against God." Joshua's voice boomed with authority. "God told me that someone took something from Jericho. We were warned to take nothing from Jericho. Everything there belongs to God. This is why we lost to Ai."

He paused, looking over the congregation.

Rahab looked around her. The people of Israel looked restless. They had daily chores to complete, and this was taking time out of their cramped schedule. They fidgeted from foot to foot. She heard a murmur move through the sea of people. *Someone* had caused this?

"Sanctify yourselves against tomorrow," Joshua continued. "In the morning, you will come before the judges – tribe by tribe. The tribe that God chooses will come before us family by family, and the family that God takes will come man by man. The man God takes shall be burnt with fire along with all that he took and all that is his."

Rahab gasped as her hand flew to her mouth. Burnt with fire? Did that mean all his children, his wife, his servants, stock, everything? Everyone? It seemed extreme.

The congregation dispersed. Tomorrow would be the day of reckoning.

Salmon attempted to sit up. Debra rushed to his side, reached behind him, and adjusted the linen pillows behind his back. She sure moved fast!

"Don't hurt my daughter," she said, her tone frank.

He looked at her with a questioning look. She stared into his eyes. Not blinking. Staring him down like she could overpower him with her will alone. He squirmed under her scrutiny.

"Don't hurt my daughter," she repeated. "She's been hurt too much already."

"I won't. I promise." Salmon waited for her to continue. She was going to say more. He could see it in her face.

"Her father." Debra looked down at her hands, clasped in front of her. She stooped down and sat beside him on the floor. "He was very controlling. Very abusive. She held up well, but it damaged her. More than you would ever know."

Salmon thought about Rahab. About her being hurt. Hurt by her own father. He began to get mad. Mad at her father.

"Then there was another man. Yassib. He was also abusive to her. Verbally so. He went out of his way to make her life miserable. Then her father betrothed her to him, knowing Yassib would hurt her more. Abuse her possibly to death. They both hated her. Her father because he couldn't break her—no matter how much he tried. And he tried hard, believe me. Yassib because she defiantly stood against him. No matter what he tried. It embarrassed him in front of his friends and family."

Salmon took a deep breath. His wound began to hurt from the tension that was building in his shoulders.

"Yassib was the reason she joined the temple," Debra continued. He could hear bitterness and hate in her voice. "He's the reason she became a temple prostitute."

Salmon nodded his head. "Yes, I know. Rahab told me."

Debra's eyes opened wide in shock, then quickly turned back into the serious glare she'd had since beginning the story.

Salmon pondered what had been said. All that had happened to her may explain why she'd always been so stand-offish. It made him wonder if that was why she had said, "Not yet." As his mind whirred, he began to understand her more than he thought he ever could.

"When she completed her contract with the temple, no one would hire her. No one cares about a harlot. No one.

"Her father disowned her when she joined the temple. He wouldn't let us near her. Her whole family had turned their back on her. All of us. He made us." She looked up at Salmon, tears in her eyes. He watched as they began to spill down her cheeks. "She's been hurt too much. Don't hurt her.

"You should know. I would kill for my daughter. I love her. Don't hurt my daughter."

Debra stood up and moved away from him back to what she had been doing. Little things here and there, waiting for Rahab to return from the assembly.

Salmon tried to lie back down. He smiled to himself. It was good to know that Debra was so protective of Rahab — that she loved her so much.

"And if you ever tell her we had this conversation," Debra called from across the tent. "I'll kill you." She smiled, but he knew she was dead serious.

No, he'd never tell her. It would be their little secret.

Chapter 22

Bilba and Lily sat at Rahab's feet drawing pictures in the sand. Rahab had just finished braiding Lily's hair the evening before while the women had sat watching Salmon sleep. The braids were made into long rows stretching from her forehead to the back of her head where the braids were pulled together in a tail. Her little head bobbed up and down, following the movement of her busy finger. Rahab was glad that Lily had found something to keep her busy.

Rahab stood quietly beside Andrew. Her hair, much of which had worked itself from its braids, kept catching the faint breeze and blowing into her face. Her mother had been very busy. Rahab hated to ask her to rebraid her hair. She hadn't found anyone else able to tightly braid it, and she wasn't good at braiding her own hair. Her back ached. Her feet hurt. She was hot, and her patience was wearing thin. She wished it was Salmon standing beside her, but he still wasn't healed enough to tolerate standing for long periods of time.

She and Andrew had been standing here for over an hour already. The tribes had marched by Joshua one by one until the tribe of Judah was taken. The family of the Zabdi of the family of the Zarhites was now coming before Joshua man by man. It was a long, drawn-out process.

Rahab looked up at Andrew. "Why?" she asked. "Why does all he has and all his family have to die? It doesn't seem right." She stood with her eyes downcast, trying to understand God.

"It's a grievous offense to take that which belongs to God."

"Yes, but why his whole family? They didn't do anything wrong."

"Wrong? He couldn't be hiding what he stole without his family knowing about it. They're as much in the wrong as he is."

"But the children?" She looked into Andrew's blue eyes, trying to find the answers hidden there.

"The guilty man is responsible for the deaths of thirty-six men. He murdered thirty-six soldiers. He committed a sin against the nation. The Torah tells us God visits the sin of the father upon the third and fourth generation. That would include his children."

Rahab looked down at Lily, her jewel. Would God hold Lily responsible for *her* sins? She had so much to account for.

Everyone stood at attention, trying to see Joshua, perking their ears up so they could better hear. Joshua had named the trespasser. It was Achan, the son of Carmi.

Achan's wife loudly wailed. "No!" She threw herself to the ground at Achan's feet, grasping them in a moment of desperation. An older woman, his mother Rahab guessed, stood beside him. She lowered her grey head, her hands clasped in front of her. Her son would die for his sins. Her grandchildren would suffer the same fate. Her shoulders shook as she began to sob. The sob turned into a wail, but she just stood where she was, head hung in despair.

Achan stood before Joshua, looking downcast and dejected. His whole body testified his guilt. His head hung in shame. His shoulders slumped forward and shook like he was gasping with big sobs.

"Achan, my son," Joshua's voice boomed, "give God the glory He deserves and confess your sin before Him and the whole congregation."

There was a long silence before a small voice spoke unto Joshua. "I've sinned against God and all of Israel. After Jericho was defeated, when we were leaving, I saw a beautiful Babylonian garment lying in the road. In its pockets were two hundred shekels of silver. Under it laid a wedge of gold of fifty shekels weight. I coveted them. And I took them." There was another pause. "They're hidden in the earth in the midst of my tent."

Joshua sent two men to search for the garment and silver and gold. They quickly returned and handed all they had retrieved to Joshua. He looked it over. Sympathy flashed across his face but was soon replaced with the sternness of a judge handing down a sentence.

Two men stepped forward and held Achan's arms, one on each side. All of Israel followed as the two soldiers led Achan and his family into a valley off to the north. All of Achan's children and a small flock of sheep and even his tent were carried along. There wasn't much—it only took a few men to carry it and a few more to herd the sheep. Nevertheless, all of Israel crowded around offering their help.

"Why have you troubled us?" Joshua asked, the voice of a leader responsible for the welfare of thousands upon thousands of people. He stood tall and proud, his chin lifted in authority, his eyes trained upon Achan. "The Lord shall trouble thee this day."

Everyone around Rahab stooped down as one to gather large stones. There were many large rocks near the valley. They hurled the rocks at Achan and all he had, burying them with a great pile of stones. Rahab turned away from the scene and turned Lily into her, planting her face into her robe and covering the back of her head with her hand. When Rahab thought it was all over, Joshua ordered the heap to be set on fire. There was plenty of material peeking out from under the stones to keep the fire going.

"Now the fierceness of God's anger has been turned away from us, and He goes with us once more." Joshua finished with a prayer of praise to God. "Almighty God, we thank You that You see our love for you and the acknowledgment of our sin as a nation. Thank You for Your great forgiveness and Your love toward us. You are the great God, the only God, the God of mercy and grace. You are our strength, our high tower, our protection, and the giver of life. You brought us out of Egypt, fought our battles for us, and have covered us in the wilderness. You are the great God of Israel. We thank You for Your grace. Amen and amen."

The people of Israel answered, "Amen," and turned to walk back to their own tents, a weight having been lifted off their shoulders.

"They're going up against Ai again!" A man shouted as he ran through the camp.

Salmon sat up on his pallet. *Too fast.* He looked to see Rahab on the far side of the tent. She was sitting with her back to him, bent over something in her lap, humming one of his favorite songs. The fact that *she* was singing it made it that much better.

She turned toward him. She saw him staring at her and smiled—a bright, full smile. She laid a small robe—*Lily's*—on the pallet beside her and practically glided over to him. She sat beside him on the pallet and laid her head on his shoulder. His eyes grew wide in amazement. He had been right! It *was* love he had heard in her voice!

She sat like that for close to a minute and then spoke, "I want to marry you." She nestled her head further into his shoulder and laid her hand on his arm.

"Why?"

"Did you change your mind? You don't want to marry me, do you?" She lifted her head off his shoulder and stared deeply into his eyes.

She wore a partially panicked expression like she'd exposed herself in the midst of a battle.

He took her soft, warm hands in his, rubbing circles on the backs with his thumbs.

"Yes, I still want to marry you. But are you sure you're ready? I don't want you to feel pushed into anything."

"I'm sure," she said. "I thought I'd lost you." Her voice caught in her throat. Her eyes welled up with tears. "I don't ever want to be without you another day in my life."

He pulled her into his arms. She laid her head back on his shoulder, and he stroked her beautiful black braids. "I'm glad because I never want to be apart from you again, either."

She sat up, pulling away from him just enough to see into his eyes. She traced her finger down his jaw line coming to rest near the cleft in his chin. She pulled his chin down just enough to line his lips up with hers, and their lips mingled into a long, passionate kiss.

Salmon listened as Israel marched off into battle. Spirits were high. They sang a song of Moses as they marched. They had turned God's judgment away, and God was going with them. God would give them the victory.

At the end of the day, Israel returned, again singing a song of praise to God, a song of Moses. Salmon heard armor clinging, barely audible over the sound of praise and triumph. Israel must have won. Yes, God had promised to fight for them.

He wondered about the battle. What had happened?

Andrew bustled into his tent and sank into the pallet beside Salmon. He sounded breathless from excitement. His eyes were bright and wide. He touched Salmon's shoulder gently, trying not to hurt him. "You missed it! It was so great!"

Salmon looked at Andrew expectantly. The excitement was contagious. He slowly nodded his head, encouraging him to go on.

"Joshua had us split up. He put about five thousand men to the west of the city to lie in wait, and the rest of us camped to the north. Ai came out against us, and Joshua had us all run—like Israel did the first time we fought Ai. Ai gathered all the men in the city to chase after Israel. Then the five thousand men ambush rose up, went into the city and burned it with fire. When Israel saw the smoke, they turned back to fight Ai. When Ai's soldiers looked back at the city and saw the smoke, they started to fall before Israel. It was like they lost heart, and I'm sure they did. Their wives and children

206

were in Ai—the Ai that was being conquered and burnt with fire. The ambush came out against the soldiers of Ai from behind. Ai was caught in between all of Israel's army! Every man of the city of Ai fell before Israel." Andrew's smile was unmatched.

In the quiet, Salmon heard the bleating of sheep and the braying of asses.

"We took everything we could out of Ai as God commanded us. Then we burnt Ai with fire and made it a heap—a desolation."

Shofars sounded. Joshua was calling all of Israel together again. Salmon slowly moved off his pallet, threw his robe around him, and ambled toward the sound of the shofar.

"You don't have to come," Andrew said. "You need to rest and heal."

"Yes, I do," Salmon said. "I've missed too much already."

Israel gathered at Mount Ebal. They watched as Joshua built an altar to God, an altar made of whole stones. Salmon had seen many altars built, altars like this one. God commanded Israel to use whole stones that hadn't been formed by any type of tool. The altar had to be made out of rough stones.

A Levite, clothed in a white linen robe with a red belt tied about his loins and a red scarf hung around his neck, brought a lamb to Joshua before the whole congregation. He placed his hand on its head. "God has given us the victory! Now we give thanks to God!"

The high priest stepped up before Joshua. His clothing was beautiful. He wore a white robe with what looked like a smaller purple robe with golden fringe hanging off the bottom edges over it. He wore a vest over that with a purple background that was covered with red diamonds. His sash was made of the same material. On the top, the very last layer, he wore a gold breastplate with twelve different colored jewels set in it. His hat was crown-like with a golden band around his head and a white, puffy material poking out high above it. There was a purple stripe of material down the center. It truly was awe-inspiring.

The priest took the lamb, a spotless, perfect lamb, and placed it upon the altar. He ceremonially sliced its throat in the way God and commanded long ago that sacrifices were to be prepared.

"Lord," the priest said loudly. "We offer this sacrifice to You in thanks for our victory today. You are the one and only great God. The God of gods. The King of kings. The ruler and protector of Israel. We offer these burnt sacrifices to You,".

The Levite stepped up and set the dead lamb on fire.

"Let the sweet scent of our thanks and praise be pleasing in Your sight," said the priest.

Salmon was glad the smoke went straight up. There had been times that the smoke drifted throughout the congregation, making eyes water and throats itch.

Joshua leaned a large flat rock up against the altar and carved in it the Law of Moses as everyone watched. This was truly a blessed time, a time God had brought to them, a time of praise to God.

Rahab took Salmon's hand as they strolled back to the tent. They were getting married. They would become one. She couldn't keep her energy bottled up. She spoke fast, bounced as she walked, and smiled like she never smiled before. Salmon looked at her with a large smile all of his own. He understood.

"So, when do you want to marry?" Salmon asked.

"The sooner, the better," Rahab said. She curved her arm through the crook of his elbow and looked into his blue eyes, almost becoming lost in the depths.

Salmon nodded his head. His lips pressed together, and his eyes creased in thought.

"I'll talk to Joshua tomorrow," he said, and his smile returned.

Chapter 23

Rahab was getting more and more nervous as the time dragged on. Salmon had left early that morning to speak to Joshua about their wedding. What was taking so long? Had Joshua said no? Was Salmon arguing their case?

What if Salmon had fallen along the way? What if he was lying in the camp somewhere, unable to go on because of his injuries? Was he really well enough yet to be making the trek all the way to Joshua's tent? What if—

The tent flap rustled then swung wide as Salmon stepped past it, his blue robe brushing the ground as he ducked inside. Rahab let out her breath. Salmon was okay. Better than okay. His smile was wide, and his steps strong and sure.

She noticed that he was standing up straight. *Miracle!* It hurt him to stand up straight just a few days before. His shoulders were jutted back, and his head was held high.

He walked up to her and, grabbed her hands and twirled her around. A flash of pain crossed his face. "Okay," he grunted, "that was a little too much."

"I'm assuming you carry good news," Rahab said. "Either that or you have completely gone crazy." She smiled at his antics.

"Good news for sure!" Salmon grabbed her hands again and pulled her into a tight embrace. "We marry tomorrow afternoon."

The next morning, Rahab woke up slowly—like usual. She stretched her arms high above her head and groaned. Above her, the tent was starting to droop from the beating of the weather. Her eyes burned, and she had a crick in her neck. She sat up on her messy pallet and tried stretching again to ease the tension from her back. It didn't work.

Suddenly, she remembered the importance of this day. Today she was marrying Salmon. One last time, she wondered why he loved her. She'd been a harlot before coming to Israel. She was an outcast of her family. She had a child who, as far as anyone in the camp knew, was her child out of wedlock. Why would anyone love *her*? But someone did. Salmon.

She jumped up from her pallet and hurried through her morning routine. She collected a pot of water from the river and washed herself. She wasn't hungry but forced herself to eat a piece of fruit—wild grapes that were collected from the edges of the Jordan River.

She woke Lily and pulled her into her lap for their cuddle time. Lily woke up, as sluggishly as Rahab in the mornings. She got Bilba and Lily their breakfast of cheese and grapes and checked her hair for loose strands. She helped Lily dress for the day, tying her sandals upon her feet. She then sent Lily and Bilba out to play with the other children, who had been up and playing for quite a while judging from the squeals and laughter that had aroused her from her pleasant dreams.

Now to do something about my hair. Rahab brushed her hand over the loose strands, feeling the frizz.

She slowly and painstakingly removed the tied strands of wool thread and took her braids out. She decided to try putting her hair up again in long braids. She was unsure if she could. She'd never tried doing her own hair before.

Debra walked in quietly and slipped up behind Rahab without her hearing her. She startled Rahab as she started to fuss her hair.

"You're so beautiful," Debra said, resting her hands on Rahab's shoulders and giving them a squeeze. "You always have been."

"That's what you always say, Mother."

"But you truly are. Salmon sees it too."

Rahab sighed, contented, and put her hands on top of her mother's.

Debra pulled her hands free and started to braid her daughter's hair.

"Do you have time to do this, Mother?"

"I do today. It's your wedding day, sweetheart. I'm here for you all day long."

"Thank you." Rahab settled in for the braiding. It usually took a long time.

An hour later, the braiding done, Rahab hugged Debra. "Thank you, Mother."

Debra squeezed her back. "I'm so happy for you, sweetheart. You marry the man you love today." She pulled away and looked at her oldest daughter and then pulled her back into a tight hug.

The afternoon was bright. A slight breeze cooled the air a little bit. Rahab looked around herself. A lone palm tree offered scant shade off to the west. Beside it, a cool spring bubbled up. Rahab smiled. God seemed to always take care of His own.

Rahab was wearing a new red robe given to her by Joshua's wife. She batted at the white veil that covered her face. She knew it was a necessity, part of the tradition, but she wished she didn't have to wear it. Her vision was somewhat limited by it, and it tickled her face.

She stood under a small canopy made of fine white linen. There were four men, Andrew and three other men Rahab didn't recognize, each holding up one of the poles that held up the wedding canopy. Lily, Bilba, and Debra stood just outside the right side of the canopy so they could easily see the ceremony.

She smiled as she saw Salmon walking toward her. His smile matched hers.

As soon as he arrived, they started the ceremony. The Levitical priest who was heading up the ceremony had walked Rahab through the entire ceremony and the different symbolisms the night before. There was a lot involved. She hoped she wouldn't forget anything she was supposed to do.

The priest, dressed all in white linen and with a tall white bonnet upon his head, held out a piece of parchment to Salmon. He took it and bent over a small table that had been set outside the canopy to sign the parchment.

"What's that for?" Rahab asked.

"This is the ketubah," Salmon explained. "By signing this, I promise to care for you."

Salmon handed it back to the priest, and the priest recited a prayer for Rahab out of Genesis, the first book of the Torah. "Thou are our sister, be thou the mother of thousands of millions, and let thy seed possess the gate of those which hate them."

Rahab was so happy she remembered what to do next. She walked around Salmon three times. She was told that the three circuits represented the virtues of marriage, which were justice, righteousness, and loving kindness.

Salmon gently took Rahab's right hand in his and slipped a ring, a slender, plain gold band, upon her right index finger. "Behold, you are consecrated to me with this ring according to the Law of Moses and Israel."

Salmon turned toward the priest. Rahab blushed. She was supposed to turn too but had forgotten as she stared at the beautiful ring Salmon had given her.

"Blessed are You, Lord, our God, sovereign of the universe, who creates the fruit of the vine," the priest said over a cup of grape juice he held in his hand. "Blessed are You, Lord, our God, sovereign of the universe, who created everything for His Glory. Blessed are You, Lord, our God, Sovereign of the universe, Who creates man. May the barren one exult and be glad as her children are joyfully gathered to her. Blessed are You, LORD, who gladden Zion with her children. Grant perfect joy to these love companions, as You did your creations in the Garden of Eden. Blessed are You, LORD, who grants the joy of groom and bride. Blessed are You, LORD, our God, sovereign of the universe, who created joy and gladness, groom and bride, mirth, song, delight and rejoicing, love and harmony, and peace and companionship. Soon, LORD our God, may there ever be heard in the cities of our Promised Land voices of joy and gladness, voices of groom and bride, the jubilant voices of those joined in marriage under the bridal canopy, the voices of young people feasting and singing. Blessed are You, LORD, who causes the groom to rejoice with his bride."

The priest handed the cup of juice to Salmon. After he took a drink; he handed it to Rahab to take a drink as well. It took her a few minutes to figure out how to get the cup up under her long veil. She looked forward to the time she would be taking it off. They handed the cup back to the priest, then Salmon took Rahab's hand and led her to his tent.

Rahab couldn't think of a time when she had ever been happier. She walked beside her husband, hand in hand. She looked back at Lily, standing beside Bilba and her meemaw, a large smile on her face. The last thing she saw before she and Salmon disappeared behind the flap of their tent was her Lily waving at her. Her beautiful Lily Rose.

"Onward to Shechem!" Someone shouted from outside the tent.

They were moving camp? Salmon sat up, rousing Rahab from her sleep.

"What's going on?" she asked.

They heard it again. "Onward to Shechem!"

"Time to tear down the tent," Salmon said, looking at Rahab. His smile lit up his face.

Rahab loved to look at him. His smiles were wide and genuine. His black hair was shorn close to his head, letting her see the perfect curve of his head. His ears were perfect. His teeth were white as sheep's wool. His eyes were like blue sapphires, deep set and twinkling. Her gaze traveled downward over his broad shoulders and his perfect, muscular chest. She reached out and traced her finger down his chest. He pulled her in close, and she laid her head on his chest. He reached up and tousled her braids.

"I love you," he said.

Rahab sighed in contentment. "I love you too. So much."

Salmon slowly let her go and stood up. He shrugged into his robe, and Rahab followed. She hugged her arms around herself and looked up at the roof of the tent.

"How do you take these things apart?" She asked. "How do you put them back together?"

"Don't worry," Salmon said. "We can do this together."

The pieces of her life were falling into order. She was no longer "Rahab, the harlot." She was "Rahab, the Israelite, the accepted of God." She was no longer someone who would never be good enough. She was someone in the shadow of God's wings, protected, and made good enough in God's eyes by His love for her.

She was no longer the pleaser of men; she was one who found true love with *one* man, a thing she never thought possible. She'd found happiness in a man worth having. One who loved her daughter as his own. She and Lily were so blessed! Where she'd once been depressed and bitter, she'd now found life worth living. She had found love.

ABOUT THE AUTHOR

Nishoni Harvey has been writing since she was a little tyke. She has honed that skill through the classes she took in obtaining her bachelor's degree in Secondary Education/English and then by taking two other intense programs through which she gained certifications through outside colleges in writing.

She has authored ten books to date, is ghostwriting yet another, and has another of her own almost completed.

She owns **Authors Aflame,** through which she helps others to write and publish their books. She has two different programs:

Author Polishing—She takes aspiring writers by the hand and leads them step-by-step, working closely with them, from mind mapping through publication! You can go from a bright idea to published in a little more than six months!

Publication Consultant—She offers her step-by-step guidance in getting your book published. Extra services can be added, like copy-editing, line editing, formatting, preparing your book cover, and marketing.

Authors Aflame also offers editing services, ghostwriting, proofreading, and more!

She has courses in writing, publication, and marketing. There also a blog to help you along, a facebook page, and a group.

For more information, visit www.authorsaflame.com.

Can You Help?

Thank You For Reading My Book!

I really appreciate all of your feedback, and I love hearing what you have to say.

I need your input to make the next version of this book and my future books better.

Please leave me an honest review on Amazon letting me know what you thought of the book.

Thanks so much!

Nishoni L Harvey

www.ingramcontent.com/pod-product-compliance
Lightning Source LLC
Chambersburg PA
CBHW020945180626
46814CB00003B/931